✳ Stardom! ✳

✳ Fame and fortune ✳
could be one step away!

Welcome to

Fame
School

For another fix of

read

Fame School

Star Maker

Cindy Jefferies

USBORNE

For Fiona Francesca Landless
a real little star!

First published in 2008 by Usborne Publishing Ltd., Usborne House,
83-85 Saffron Hill, London EC1N 8RT, England. www.usborne.com

A CIP catalogue record for this book is available from the British Library.

JFMA JJASOND/08

ISBN 9780746097151

Printed in Great Britain.

1 The Winners Return

"Look! They've put up a banner!" said Tara, clutching Chloe's arm with excitement.

They peered out of the minibus window as it drew up outside Rockley Park School. Tara was right. A huge, white sign was hanging above the main door. *Welcome back, Winners!* it said in large, black writing. Underneath, in smaller letters, were all their names: *Chloe, Danny, Ed, Ben* and of course *Tara*. And standing underneath the banner, crowded around the front door, were loads of students and members of staff, all waving and cheering.

Tara and her friends in the band, Wizard Monkey Breath Scares the Horses, had just won the

International Battle of the Bands competition in Italy, which had been televised all over the world. No wonder they were getting such an enthusiastic welcome back at school! Rockley Park existed to train people who wanted to make it in the music industry, and this win was wonderful for the school *and* the band. So, as well as all the cheering students and teachers, Mrs. Sharkey, the Principal, was waiting to greet the winners.

"Congratulations!" she said as Tara and the rest of the band got out of the minibus. Tara had never seen such a broad smile on the head teacher's face before. "You've done us all proud," Mrs. Sharkey continued. "I know everyone wants to hear all about it, so there will be a special assembly tomorrow morning just for you."

"Really?" Tara felt pleased. There were bound to be all sorts of questions from staff and students, so it would be good to have some time set aside to answer them. After all, the band's experience might help people who wanted to enter the competition next year.

"I'll conduct a question-and-answer session with

you," Mrs. Sharkey told them. "And of course we'll all want to hear you play 'Sky Blue' again." She beamed at her students. "You must be tired after your journey," she said. "We've kept a late tea for you, so come in and have something to eat."

Tara didn't feel that hungry. The meal on the plane had been okay, but she was looking forward to a drink. As they made their way indoors, lots of excited students called out to them.

"Congratulations!"

"You sounded fantastic!"

"Go, Wizard Monkey Breath!"

"Great drumming, Danny!"

"Well done!"

"You did it, Tara!"

An older student, grinning broadly, slapped Tara enthusiastically on her back. She wasn't sure how to react. It was very different from being onstage, responding to a cheering crowd. These were her fellow students, and she wasn't used to being so popular with them. She didn't want to be thought big-headed, but she couldn't avoid a happy smile filling her face.

However, Mrs. Sharkey didn't want the winners mobbed, or the rest of her students to get overexcited. "I think these poor travellers need a chance to catch their breath," she told the crowd sternly. "You'll hear about their trip in the morning. Off you go now. Let them have their tea in peace."

Nobody dared to disagree. The crush eased and soon Tara and the band found themselves sitting in the quiet dining room, enjoying their tea with Judge Jim and Mr. and Mrs. Player, the adults who had accompanied the band on their trip. After all the excitement of the competition, and the journey back, it *was* good to have a bit of peace at last, although the welcome home had been fantastic.

"It feels weird to be back here," said Tara, taking in the familiar surroundings. "We were only away for three days, but it seems like a long time."

"Well a lot has happened in those three days," said Judge Jim. "Foreign travel, rehearsals, your wonderful performance. It'll take a little while to feel normal again."

"But I'm sure Mrs. Sharkey will want to get you back to your schoolwork as soon as possible," added Mr. Player. They all laughed.

After a long drink, and a nibble of cake, Tara was ready to go to her room to unpack. Everyone else was busy with homework in their boarding houses, so it did seem rather odd to be sitting in the large, empty dining room.

"I'm going over to see Marmalade," said Danny, draining his glass. "It feels as if I haven't spoken to him in ages."

Marmalade Stamp was a dancer. He was Danny's best friend and shared a room with him, Ed and Ben. Tara couldn't imagine him wanting to wait even five minutes to hear all Danny's news.

Ben pushed back his chair. "I'll come with you," he said.

"Me too," said Ed.

Tara piled her plate and mug on the tray and stood up. "Coming, Chloe?" she asked. "I fancy going back to our room."

"Okay. I need to phone Mum and Dad," Chloe said, jumping up as well.

Back in the girls' boarding house it was quiet, because everyone else was still in the homework room, but after a few minutes Pop and Lolly, their other two roommates, burst in.

"Did you like the banner?" asked Pop, excitedly. "We just had time to do it before you got back."

Pop and Lolly had been in the audience at the competition with their mother, and had got an earlier flight home.

"It was brilliant!" said Tara. "Thanks ever so much."

"What was your day like after we left?" asked Lolly.

"We had to do a photo shoot with the other winners," said Tara. "And there were a couple of interviews, but that was about it really."

"We had a lovely, relaxing lunch and a swim before we had to go to the airport," said Chloe, after closing her phone. "It was great. Like being on holiday!"

"Better than us," grumbled Pop. "I hate getting to an airport when it's still dark in the morning. I can't *believe* how early we had to get up."

"But now we're all back to normal," said Tara.

"*We* might be," said Pop with a laugh. "But *you* won't."

"What do you mean?" asked Tara.

"Well for a start there's that special assembly in the morning," Pop told her. "Mrs. Sharkey said she's going to interview you all, as if you're on TV. And then there are bound to be real TV interviews, press coverage, all sorts of things. You didn't think you'd be able to disappear back into obscurity, did you?"

"Wow!" said Chloe. "Is there really a lot of interest in us?"

"Well, you're in all the papers," said Lolly. "I should have brought them from the common room. I'll go and get them in a moment."

"No, don't!" said Tara before she could stop herself.

"Why ever not?" asked Pop.

"Yes, what's the matter?" asked Chloe. "It's really exciting. Don't you want to read about yourself in the newspapers?"

Tara looked at her friends. Pop and Lolly were staring at her with puzzled expressions on their faces. The twins were both used to the limelight, because they had already released one single, and were successful fashion models too. And as for Chloe, Tara knew that her ambition had always been to be a pop star, and everyone understood what attention that might bring. But although Tara loved to perform, she'd never been particularly interested in the glitz and glamour of stardom. How could she explain that without sounding like a spoilsport?

Tara shrugged. "Okay," she agreed. "Get the newspapers if you like. I'm not bothered. It's just that I've always been more interested in making music than headlines."

"Tara! How can you be so pompous?" squealed Pop.

Chloe looked almost as scandalized. "Honestly, Tara!" she complained. "*You* might not care about a bit of publicity, but I do. I've never even had my name in the *local* paper before! Go on Lolly. Please fetch them. I can't *wait* to see what they say!"

2 Rave Reviews

In a few minutes Lolly had dashed to the common room and come back with several newspapers. There was plenty to satisfy Chloe. And although the articles weren't huge, the band's win certainly hadn't gone un-noticed. Tara glanced at one of the articles. *WIZARD MONKEY BREATH SCARES THE OPPOSITION*, was the headline. *Wizard Monkey Breath Scares the Horses might be an odd name,* the article went on, *but that didn't spoil Rockley Park's chances at the recent International Battle of the Bands competition. The band went on to win their section against stiff competition, to take home the glory for the prestigious music and dance school. The good-looking band, a traditional line-up of drums, bass and two guitars, showcased the rare talents of young singer Clare Tompkins, who did justice to the surprisingly mature composition by bassist Tara Fitzgerald.*

"They got my name wrong!" said Chloe, crossly. Even so, Tara could see that she was glowing with the compliment.

"You're a *rare talent*!" Lolly read out with a smile. "Quite right too, Chloe. You are."

"And don't worry about the name being wrong," Pop told Chloe. "It happens all the time."

"You see, it's a waste of time reading newspaper articles," said Tara, feeling rather smug. "They always get things wrong."

"Like your *surprisingly mature composition*?" laughed Pop.

"Yes," growled Tara, feeling more cross than she wanted to admit. "Why did they have to say it was surprising?"

Everyone laughed, and Tara let go of her annoyance. She'd amused everyone, which gave her a good feeling, and she had enjoyed reading the article, in spite of what she'd said. A couple of the papers had made some really good comments about her songwriting ability, and that really *did* give Tara a buzz.

In spite of all the excitement, when bedtime came Tara was ready for a good night's sleep, and so were Pop and Lolly after their early morning start. Chloe was a bit late turning her light out because she was re-reading one of the newspaper articles.

"Don't keep reading that," Tara teased her, "or you'll get big-headed."

Chloe went pink with embarrassment and stuffed the paper into her drawer.

"Don't worry," Tara relented with a grin. "If you ever *did* we'd soon bring you back down to earth."

"And, Chloe, you're the most modest person I know," added Lolly firmly. "You *enjoy* those articles. You deserve a bit of glory."

In the morning they all hurried over to the main building for breakfast. Tara ate quickly. She wanted to make sure her Rickenbacker bass had been delivered safely back to the Rock Department, especially as they would have to perform their song soon. Usually she liked to take care of her guitar herself, but with the welcoming committee outside the school yesterday she hadn't had a chance. She hoped Judge Jim had put the band's instruments away.

"Going over to the Rock Department?" she asked Danny as soon as she saw him with Ed and Ben. They were all munching their way through enormous bowls of cereal.

"What for?" asked Danny.

"To check our instruments, of course," she told him. "We have to perform soon, at this special assembly thing Mrs. Sharkey told us about, so we need to get them set up."

"They aren't in the Rock Department," Ed told her through a mouthful of cornflakes. Tara felt a stab of fright. Her Rickenbacker meant an awful lot to her. Her parents had given it to her as a surprise present. Surely it couldn't have gone missing?

"Calm down, Tara," said Danny, as her eyes opened

wide with concern. "Some of the older students have set our kit up onstage in the hall with Judge Jim, so it's ready for us. You don't have to worry about a thing."

"It's like having roadies," said Ben with a grin. "Isn't it great?"

"I suppose so," admitted Tara. She could certainly trust Judge Jim to get things right. She contented herself by scowling at Ed for alarming her. But she couldn't stay cross for long because he made silly faces at her disapproving frown.

Soon after breakfast, everyone filed into the hall for the special assembly. Onstage, the band's kit had indeed been set up for them, and in front of the equipment were six chairs and a low table ready for their interview. There was a buzz of anticipation around the room, but as soon as Mrs. Sharkey appeared everyone fell silent.

"This assembly is both to congratulate our winning students and to give them an opportunity to answer questions about their experience," she said. "As you know, this is the first time Rockley Park has entered the

International Battle of the Bands competition. So I hope they've brought back a few tips as well as lots of happy memories. Please welcome Chloe, Tara, Danny, Ed and Ben!"

Tara and the rest of the band went up onstage to loud cheers and applause. Mrs. Sharkey showed them to their seats and the question-and-answer session began.

Tara didn't feel very comfortable speaking to an audience. She felt strange without her bass to hold on to. But she was in familiar surroundings. Rockley Park was a small school; it really couldn't have been a less threatening environment. And Tara did want to share her experience. Some of the things Wizard Monkey Breath had learned might well help another band in the future.

They talked about the competition venue and setting up their equipment. Danny mentioned taking his own snare drum and Chloe spoke about using all the space on the vast stage. There were questions about rehearsals, technical help, their competitors and much more. Eventually someone asked a question about the song they had performed.

"Did the actual song make much difference, do you think?" he asked. "Or was your look and how you sounded more important?"

The band members looked at each other and Ed stepped in to reply.

"I guess you'd have to ask the judges that," he said, and everyone in the audience laughed.

"The whole package was important. I'm sure of that," said Chloe. "If we hadn't made a huge effort with the way we looked, for instance, we'd have seemed amateurish next to the others. But Tara's song was vital too."

Ben broke in. "The song was perfect for our sound, especially with Chloe's voice," he said. "We couldn't have done it without the song."

"As the songwriter, do you have anything to add?" Mrs. Sharkey asked Tara.

Tara shrugged. "Well, we had to perform an original song," she told the audience. "So I suppose it was part of the test. But I didn't try to match the song to the band, or anything like that. It was just something I'd been working on for a while and it seemed to fit the bill. Everyone liked it and so we decided to use it. We were just lucky I guess."

"Well I think we'll let that modest response end our session," said Mrs. Sharkey. "In a few minutes I want you all to go quietly to your lessons, but first, Wizard Monkey Breath are going to reprise that winning song for you. Here they are, performing 'Sky Blue'."

A few senior students ran onstage to clear away the table and chairs and the band went to their instruments. Chloe picked up her microphone and waited for Danny to start them off. Soon, the "Sky Blue" tune flooded out into the hall, as Ben played the first few bars.

The band knew the song so well they played it almost faultlessly. Tara found herself drifting through it, because a germ of an idea for a new song was fluttering at the edge of her mind, making demands on her concentration.

As the final chords faded away Chloe came up to Tara and gave her a hug. All the students in the audience were clapping like mad, and Tara felt very pleased with her performance. But at the same time she itched to get away and write her new song idea down before she forgot it. Who knew, it might even turn out to be more popular than "Sky Blue"!

3 Exciting News

As soon as morning lessons were over, Tara went to her favourite quiet corner, and started to work on her new song. She hastily scribbled down the words that had been on her mind. They would need developing, of course, but she was sure she was onto something good.

She felt a burst of excitement. It was different from the feelings she had before she went onstage. That was excitement mixed with fear, as well as determination to do her best. But this was a kind of wild exhilaration, which came bubbling up from inside her. She had no idea where her ideas came from. Sometimes the words came first, and sometimes just a fragment of tune, but this time she could hear the notes *and* words in her mind at once.

She simply *had* to write down these ideas when they came, because if she didn't they could disappear altogether. That had happened some time ago, with a different tune. She had found, to her dismay, that by the time she went into the small recording studio in school to capture it on CD, much of it had disappeared from her mind. Now, she made a point of putting her ideas on paper as soon as she could. She even had a special little paper-covered notebook, which had a mixture of plain and music manuscript paper in it, so she could easily scribble down some notes and words at the same time. But first, she had to let the tune develop a bit more in her mind. So, when a senior student came up to her and broke her chain of thought, Tara felt cross.

"Message from Mrs. Sharkey," the student told her. "She wants to see you in her office right away."

Tara bit back her annoyance. It wasn't the student's fault she would have to stop working on the song. She thanked the student and hastily used the manuscript paper to draw the notes for the riff that was in her mind. That would have to do until she could get to her bass. In fact, what she *really* needed was an acoustic guitar to develop tunes on. She could keep it in her room, and use it whenever she had a spare moment. She'd have to ask her parents for one for her birthday, but meanwhile she had to get to the Principal's office. She slid the notebook into her back pocket, and made her way reluctantly upstairs.

Tara knocked and went in. She was surprised to see that the rest of Wizard Monkey Breath was there as well, and then she felt a bit silly. If she hadn't been so involved with her songwriting she might have guessed that it would be something to do with the band.

Chloe gave her a wide smile. "There's exciting news!" she told Tara.

"There is indeed," agreed the Principal. "But we have to take a measured approach. You see," she told Tara, "I've been getting quite a few calls since your win, inviting the band to appear at various events. Amongst other things you've been asked to appear on TV, and to play at various gigs and summer festivals. Obviously there's your schoolwork to consider. You won't be able to do everything, and it would be a mistake to try. But I just wanted to let you know that invitations are beginning to come in, and to check that you're all happy to make at least some appearances."

Tara glanced at the others. They all looked incredibly pleased at the attention they were getting. It was turning out to be just as Pop had predicted.

"It's great, isn't it?" Ben said to Tara. "One competition win and we're famous!"

"Steady on," warned Mrs. Sharkey. "You all need to think about this carefully. Do any of you actually want to base your careers on Wizard Monkey Breath?"

The friends exchanged glances. "Well…" said Chloe slowly. "It's fantastic singing with the band…and I certainly don't want to turn anything down, but I always thought I'd concentrate on a solo career really…"

"Out of choice I'd usually play more heavy stuff,"

ventured Ed. "But it's fantastic getting all this attention!"

The others nodded. "We came together for the competition," Tara pointed out. "I'd rather be a songwriter than a performer really. But I agree with the others. We can't refuse all these requests. It would be mean!"

"Fine," said Mrs. Sharkey. "That's what I thought. In which case we must manage your success with that in mind. It'll be fun for you to bask in this popularity, and it will give you some valuable performing experience. Of course, I'll be keeping your parents informed at all times about what is going on."

Mrs. Sharkey peered at them over the thick-rimmed glasses she'd recently taken to wearing.

"Once something else newsworthy comes along in the music world you'll be in less demand," she went on. "And then we can let the band fade out quietly if that's what you want. But do enjoy yourselves while this lasts. Being able to handle the media well is an important part of your education."

"Well if it's part of our education we'd *definitely*

better do these gigs and appearances, hadn't we?" said Tara wryly. "As long as I have time to write my songs as well, I'll be happy."

"Right then. I'll wait and see what other invitations we get over the next couple of days and then I'll put an itinerary together for you," said Mrs. Sharkey. "It'll mean having to catch up on some of your schoolwork later, but I'm sure you'll think it's worth that. For now, I want you to concentrate on your lessons. Remember, there's no room for prima donnas at Rockley Park!"

The band members went back downstairs, chatting happily.

"I didn't think we'd get all this attention when we first entered the competition," said Ben.

"We wouldn't have done if we'd lost," Danny pointed out.

"That's true," said Chloe. "But we won! And I'm going to enjoy every moment of our fame!"

"As long as we don't get loads of journalists peering into our practice rooms while I'm trying to learn a difficult riff," said Ben. "That would be really annoying."

Tara laughed. "I don't think we're quite *that* famous," she told him. "Besides, can you see Mrs. Sharkey allowing journalists onto the school grounds?"

Chloe giggled. "No way!"

They soon got back into the rhythm of school, and over the next couple of days Tara did manage to spend some time on her new song. On a lovely sunny afternoon she went out into the garden to work. She'd got the main riff in her head now, and was working on the words. The first verse had gone well but the second verse was proving troublesome. So she wasn't too pleased at being interrupted.

"Excuse me." It was a year seven student peering at her shyly from under a long blonde fringe.

"What?" said Tara grumpily. She'd almost got the first line, but then the words had slipped away with the intrusion.

"My name's Carly," said the girl. "And I wondered if your band would sign your autographs for me. I saw you on TV when you won the competition. I wanted to ask you first because I play bass like you and…you're my hero."

Tara looked at Carly in surprise. "I can't sign autographs for you," she told her. "Mrs. Sharkey doesn't approve of that sort of thing in school." Carly looked so disappointed that Tara felt she had to add something. "Look, if you want a bass-playing hero, try Judge Jim Henson," she advised. "He's the business."

"He's not a bass player like us," objected Carly, looking puzzled.

"Oh yes he is," Tara assured her. "Okay, so he's most famous for his lead-guitar playing, but he plays bass too. I bet he'd love it if you asked him to play a bit for you."

"Really?"

"Really. Believe me. He's up there with the best of them. And I bet if you ask *him* for his autograph he'll agree."

Tara had to smile as Carly scurried off towards the Rock Department. Judge Jim would laugh, but he never minded signing autographs for star-struck year sevens. They always grew out of it eventually.

But talking to Carly had chased all the words she'd been thinking about out of Tara's head, so she packed her little notebook into her bag and slung it over her shoulder. She headed for the Rock Department, to work on the tune a bit more. If she dawdled, maybe Carly would have left by the time Tara arrived.

"Hi, Tara!" It was Charlie Owen, who was in Tara's class, and a drummer like Danny. "Fending off your fans?"

Tara laughed. "Something like that," she admitted.

"It's about time you lot stopped encouraging them," Charlie told her in an aggrieved voice.

Tara looked at him in surprise. "We haven't encouraged anyone," she told him, feeling rather put out. "I can't help it if a year seven wants to ask for my autograph – and I didn't give it to her."

But Charlie didn't look satisfied. "You're not the only talented people here, you know," he told her. "You've been back three days now but you're still behaving like celebrities."

"No we're not!" Tara felt really hurt by Charlie's accusation. Then a thought occurred to her. "You're not jealous of our success, are you?" she asked. "You don't need to be, you know."

"Huh! I wouldn't have joined your manufactured band if you'd asked me," he snapped. He headed off in the direction of the boys' boarding house and Tara watched him go.

Charlie was being rather unfair. Most of the members of Wizard Monkey Breath had been playing together for ages. It was only the addition of Chloe that had been new for the competition. But there was nothing wrong in that. And Tara was sure that Charlie would have jumped at the opportunity to be in the band if he'd been given the chance. But although he was a good drummer, Charlie had always been overshadowed by Danny, who was brilliant. That was tough, but others in the class had been overlooked and had dealt with the disappointment. Trust Charlie to be the one to make a fuss.

Tara wondered how he would have behaved if he

had been in the winning band. He'd probably have been unbearably big-headed! But she didn't want to waste time worrying about Charlie's jealousy. She needed to play her new riff. Maybe that would help her come up with a cracking second verse for the song. At this time of day the Rock Department should be fairly quiet.

When she arrived, Tara found she was right. There was no one about. She put her bag down and went over to her bass on its stand in the corner of the main practice room. The room was big, large enough to hold quite a few musicians while they jammed together. This was where Wizard Monkey Breath had practised, before flying out to Italy, and it was one of Tara's favourite places in the school.

She plugged in, put the guitar strap over her shoulder and lost herself in her new song.

After she'd been playing for a few minutes, Judge Jim appeared from his office along the corridor. He was holding a pair of wire strippers and a length of cable. He smiled at her, and she stopped playing.

"That a new song you're workin' on?" he asked.

"Yes." Tara returned his smile. "I think it's my favourite thing in the whole world, writing songs."

"Even better than performin'?"

Tara put her head on one side and considered. "Well performing is great," she admitted. "But writing songs is more exciting."

Judge Jim laughed. "I can think of a few people who wouldn't agree with you," he said. "But I know what you mean. And you have quite a talent, Tara. Your songs are really somethin'. You stick with it."

"I will," Tara assured him. "I'm going to spend all weekend working on this until it's perfect! But..." She looked at him hopefully. "I could do with an acoustic guitar in my room, to work out tunes more easily. You don't have an old one I could borrow, do you?"

Judge Jim smiled. "I'm sure I do," he told her. "Hang on." He disappeared into his office and came back with a rather battered-looking guitar. Tara could see that one of the strings was broken, but Judge Jim also had a packet of strings in his hand.

"Brilliant!" said Tara, happily. "Thanks. It'll do me fine until I get a chance to ask my dad for one."

"Will you be okay stringing an acoustic?" Judge Jim asked. Tara nodded and he laughed. "Of course you will," he agreed. "Tara Fitzgerald, never beaten by anythin'! Don't forget the rule about instruments in bedrooms, will you?" he warned her.

"I know," she said. "Don't annoy anyone else, and stop playing immediately if I'm asked."

"Good. Do you want me to call your father about gettin' an acoustic guitar of your own?"

"Yes please!" Judge Jim and Tara's father were old friends. Tara knew how difficult it could be to contact her father during the day, especially when he was working as a session musician in a recording studio. Judge Jim would be able to ring him late at night, when Tara should be fast asleep. And Judge Jim would know exactly what to ask for on her behalf.

After a bit more work on her song, Tara started to feel hungry. Several older students arrived for a jam session, having had their tea, and so she decided to call it a day. She put her bass back onto its stand, and went over to the dining room with her new instrument. Chloe, Pop and Lolly weren't there, but Danny and Ben were.

"Hey! Have you checked your pigeonhole today?" asked Ben, giving the guitar a sideways look, as she joined them with a tray of food.

Tara shook her head. "Nope," she said. "I only do that every few days. It's not as if I get loads of post or anything." She sat down and started to eat.

"Well you ought to go and check," Danny told her. He sounded really excited. "We've each had a huge bundle of post. People have been sending us fan mail!"

"It's *brilliant*!" said Ben, grinning from ear to ear. "Cards and letters and invitations. All sorts of stuff. It's like having an extra birthday! We told the girls when they came in for tea and they went rushing off to have a look. I expect they're opening Chloe's now!"

"Really?" Tara ate as quickly as she could. She wanted to be with the girls, sharing in the fun. Fan mail! It hadn't occurred to any of them that the competition win would lead to this! She abandoned the pudding and swallowed her drink as quickly as she could. Then she pushed her chair back and got up.

"Are you off, then?" said Danny. "That was quick. You haven't had any pudding yet, or explained why you've got that old guitar with you."

"I'll grab an apple on the way out," Tara told him. "The guitar is for songwriting. I'll tell you about it later."

"Have fun!" Ben called after her as she left. She waved her apple at him and almost collided with an older student who was carrying a laden tray.

"Sorry!" said Tara, still grinning at the thought of getting fan mail. She headed out of the dining room and towards her room. Tara couldn't *wait* to see her very own heap of post!

4 Fan Mail

But by the time she reached the boarding house, Tara was beginning to feel a bit anxious. What if Chloe and the boys had loads of letters but she didn't have any? After all, she was the bassist, and people might not have noticed her very much. What if no one had sent her anything? She'd feel terrible. Just because the others had fan mail, it didn't automatically follow that she would too.

As she stepped indoors she was feeling really nervous, and it didn't help when she looked into her pigeonhole and found it empty. She went along to her room with her stomach tied up in knots. From being on top of the world, she'd become anxious and worried.

She pushed the door open to see Chloe surrounded by a sea of envelopes, cards and letters. She almost backed out again, but it was too late – Chloe, Pop and Lolly had seen her.

"Tara!" said Chloe, beaming all over her face. "Come and have a look at all this!"

"We put yours on your bed!" said Lolly.

"Hurry up!" yelled Pop. "We can't wait to see what you've got."

Tara glanced at her bed and sighed with relief. She could feel her smile returning. It was all right, she *did* have a bundle of post too. Thank goodness! She felt relieved, and rather surprised that it mattered so much to her.

"Isn't this *amazing*?" said Chloe, looking up from the large card in her hand. "Look! This is from all the children at a primary school in Kent!"

She held the card out and Tara took it. It was home-made, with a drawing of Chloe singing on the front. Inside it said: *Congratulations from everyone in Class 2, Deckle Primary School, Kent.*

"Come on, open yours!" urged Pop, bouncing over to join Tara on her bed.

"I won't have anything like that," muttered Tara. "I'm only the bassist."

She sat on her bed and opened the first envelope. Inside was a postcard of a very famous rock bassist. On the back it said, *Go Tara!* Pop giggled and Tara felt really proud and pleased. It was fantastic to be appreciated, even though this card had no return address, or any clue as to who had sent it.

There were lots of bought and home-made cards, paintings and drawings, badges and even small gifts, as well as quite a few letters. Tara had never had anything like as many envelopes to open before! Chloe had even more, but that was to be expected because she was the lead singer. It took ages to go through them all, and Tara's apple lay forgotten under the heap of mail.

"How about this?" she said at last, coming across a plain, business envelope. "Did you get one of these, Chloe?"

Chloe nodded. "It's from the local music shop in

town," she said. "They want us to open a new extension to their shop. Wasn't it nice of them to send us individual letters?"

"What would we have to do?" wondered Tara aloud, hanging a little bass guitar on a chain, which someone had sent, around her neck.

"Just cut a ribbon and look glamorous, I expect," Lolly told her. "I don't suppose you'd have to say much."

"Much? I wouldn't want to say *anything*," said Tara.

"I'm sure you could manage '*I declare this shop extension open*'," giggled Pop, handing her a home-made badge that said *Tara the Star* in wonky writing. Tara pinned it to her T-shirt.

"Oh! There's a note here from Mrs. Sharkey as well," said Chloe. "I nearly missed it."

"What does it say?" asked Lolly.

Chloe scanned the note quickly. "It's our itinerary," she said. "She wants to talk us through it later, but it's nice to have the list now."

Tara scrabbled through her own pile of mail and

found her copy. "There's the local music festival tomorrow afternoon," she said. "They'd like us to go and play 'Sky Blue' because of our recent success. That should be fun. Oh, and we've been invited to be guests on *Monday Madness*! We have to go to record it on Sunday. That's brilliant!"

"*Monday Madness* is *such* a fun TV programme," said Pop, wistfully. "I wish *I* could go on it."

"What else is there?" asked Lolly.

"The shop opening is next," said Chloe, "on the following Friday afternoon. We might have to miss a lesson to do that."

"And the day after, it's a local TV news programme," said Tara. "But that's just an interview. They don't want us to play."

"A school's music day at a shopping mall midweek, and then a three-day summer festival...gosh, that's miles away. Lucky it's a Saturday," said Chloe.

"But look at the last gig on the itinerary!" said Tara. She gulped, and stared at Chloe, suddenly feeling apprehensive. "They want us to perform 'Sky Blue' at

Singing for the World." She looked at Chloe, who stared back at her with her mouth open.

"It's that *huge* charity gig they have every year in London, the one that's always shown on TV all round the world," explained Tara.

"I know what it *is*," said Chloe. "I just can't believe that *we're* going to be part of it."

For a moment there was silence in the room.

"It's in a massive outdoor arena," Pop said at last.

"Yes," said Tara, still feeling dazed. She had to read the last entry on the itinerary again before she could quite believe it. "And Singing for the World is the day after the festival on the Saturday. Wow! What a weekend *that's* going to be."

"Well. Singing for the World. Congratulations!" said Lolly, looking seriously impressed. "Famous TV stars and actors and singers take turns to introduce the acts, don't they? It's the event of the year!"

"You'll be even *more* famous after that," squealed Pop. "Everyone who's *anyone* goes along, and everyone else watches on TV!"

The thought of appearing at such an important event made Tara feel quite solemn. She'd always been a tremendous fan of charity gigs, and had even organized one herself in the past. But Singing for the World was a *huge* event. It had been started a few years earlier by some of the most famous performers in the music business. Every year it had grown and grown. Would they be up to it? Since they'd won the competition, expectations would be very high, so they mustn't let the organizers down. This event was much more than a gig, as the charity depended on the money raised every year, and if they performed really well they might even help to break last year's record takings.

Tara was pretty sure they would be performing early in the day. The *real* megastars would get top billing during the latter part of the evening. But even so, any new band would *kill* for a chance like this. They would have to make sure they were absolutely perfect on the day. It was a big responsibility.

"You've also been invited to several parties and gigs in Italy, and someone's birthday party in Poland," said

Pop, who was rifling through the opened post again.

"But I don't suppose you'll be allowed to go to them," Lolly pointed out. "Those invitations are mostly from children. They're not official, serious invitations for proper events, and they're not on your itinerary."

"We'd better have a band rehearsal tomorrow morning, before the afternoon gig at the festival," mused Chloe. "So we keep sharp."

"How many songs will we be expected to do?" asked Tara anxiously.

"I think everyone will just want 'Sky Blue'," Chloe told her. "So a quick run-through should do it."

"That's okay then," said Tara, with relief. "We can manage that in our sleep."

"Even so, we ought to have a run-through," insisted Chloe.

"I know!" said Tara impatiently. She pushed her mail to one side. "What do we do with all this?" she asked. It was wonderful to have been sent so much, but now she felt a bit like a Christmas tree, festooned with all the badges and bits and pieces. Someone had even sent them each a rather cool beanie, with a picture of a monkey wearing a wizard's hat on it!

"Well I'm going to write and thank all the people who put addresses on their cards," said Chloe.

Tara groaned. "But if you do that they'll write back and thank you for your thank you letter, and it'll go on for ever!" she said.

"Why don't you ask Mrs. Sharkey what to do when you see her?" suggested Lolly.

"Good idea," agreed Chloe.

Tara sorted through all the post, and picked out some cards she particularly liked. She put them on her bedside table, and stuffed the empty envelopes into the overflowing waste-paper basket. She squeezed the rest of the cards and letters carefully into a drawer to look at later. She couldn't wait to show them all to her parents at the end of term!

"What are you doing for the end-of-term concert?" she asked Pop, opening the packet of strings Judge Jim had given her.

"Lolly and I are doing a song together, as usual," Pop

told her. "We found a really old one from the nineteen-thirties that we *love*. We're going to make it sound as retro as possible, and dress in thirties clothes and everything. It'll be so cool. How about you?"

"Yes, are you lot going to perform 'Sky Blue'?" said Lolly.

Tara glanced over at Chloe, and Chloe shot her a questioning look. "To be honest, I'd rather not," said Tara, thoughtfully. "We'll have done it to death once we've done all these gigs and appearances. I'd rather perform something different. In fact I was thinking of playing my new song, if I ever get a chance to finish it. I'm going to make it into really heavy rock for a change." She sighed, struggling a bit to get the broken E string off the guitar. "That's what this guitar is for," she explained. "To help me work out the tune. I thought I'd ask the boys to perform it with me."

"Great!" said Chloe. "I was wondering about the band too. I was hoping to sing a solo for the end-of-term concert. I don't know what yet, but I don't think it would be fair to the rest of the students for us to expect to be able to perform 'Sky Blue' again. Not that it isn't a brilliant song," she added, hastily. "But it would be a bit of a cop-out."

"I agree," said Tara. "Excellent! Let's hope the boys feel the same."

The next day was Saturday, and there was just time for a quick rehearsal in the Rock Department. To her amusement, Tara saw that each member of the band was wearing their Wizard Monkey Breath beanie hats.

As soon as Tara mentioned her new song, the boys agreed about performing something different.

"I like 'Sky Blue', Tara. Don't get me wrong," Ed told her. "But I fancy playing some heavy rock again."

"Sounds good to me," agreed Ben. "How about you, Danny?"

As always, Danny was happy to play almost anything, but even he felt in need of a change. "It's been a while since I played any really heavy stuff," he said. "I wouldn't mind doing a bit of that. It would give everyone a blast."

"I'm glad Wizard Monkey Breath won't be appearing at the school concert," said Chloe. "You can have too much of a good thing."

Charlie appeared as they piled out of the Rock Department to wait for the minibus after their rehearsal.

"What do you look like!" he snorted at the sight of their beanies. "And what's all this about?" he sneered, poking a finger at the badge Ed was wearing.

"They were presents," said Ed, mildly.

"From fans," added Ben, with a smile. "So it's only polite to wear them, isn't it?"

"You just can't get over yourselves, can you?" said Charlie. "Tara the Star?" he laughed, looking at the home-made badge on Tara's T-shirt. "How ridiculous."

"Not as ridiculous as you," said Tara, who easily lost her temper.

"Ignore him," said Chloe quietly, as the minibus arrived. "He's only jealous."

"I can't *imagine* what it would be like to be in a band with Charlie Owen," said Tara, as they all scrambled on board. "He always has to shoot his mouth off, whatever the occasion."

"Well, fortunately, you won't have to find out." Danny smiled. "Because I'm not planning on resigning any time soon!"

"Thank goodness for that!" said Tara, with feeling, leaning back in her seat. "I know I shouldn't let Charlie get to me. The rest of you don't." She sighed, and calmed down. "After all, life is almost perfect. We have some cool gigs and appearances coming up, especially Singing for the World, we have a load of fans, and I'm making good music with my friends. I'm even full of ideas for new songs! What could possibly be better than that?"

5 Monday Madness

The festival went well, and as they only had to perform "Sky Blue", it wasn't long before they were in the minibus again, and on their way back to school.

"That was fun," said Ben. "We got a good cheer, didn't we?"

"Did you notice the local radio station van with the huge aerial?" said Chloe, excitedly. "Do you think they broadcast our performance?"

"I think they were broadcasting most of the performances," said Ben.

"That's pretty cool!" said Chloe.

Ed grinned. "I wonder if anyone at school heard it," he said.

"No doubt Charlie will have done," said Danny, with a wry smile. "And, if he did, I'm sure he'll let us know how awful we sounded."

"Ignore him," said Chloe. "This weekend is far too much fun to let Charlie spoil it. Remember, we have a TV recording tomorrow. Think about that instead. I'm really looking forward to it, aren't you, Tara?"

"Mm?" Tara was hard at work, jotting down a few words that had just come into her head. "Can you think of a good rhyme for *serious*?" she asked.

"No I can't!" said Chloe. "Why not think of an easier word?"

"I could change it round a bit," Tara admitted.

"You won't be able to spend all day scribbling in your notebook tomorrow," Chloe told her. "We're going to be in the TV studio, recording *Monday Madness*."

Monday Madness was a children's TV programme. It was a magazine programme with lots of different items, and each week a different guest was invited on. Not only would the band play "Sky Blue", they would also be interviewed by the presenter, and take part in the custard-pie fight that closed every show.

"Don't worry, Chloe," said Tara. "I'll leave my notebook at school tomorrow. I don't fancy getting it covered in custard pies. Anything can happen on *Monday Madness*!"

Mr. Player had volunteered to take them to the studio, and he was in a T-shirt and jeans when he brought the minibus to the main building for them the next morning.

"I know you lot," he teased, when they were all on board. "It would be just like you to save a custard pie for me, after the recording is over."

"I hadn't thought about that," said Ben. "Good idea!"

The recording was great fun. There were loads of children in the audience, and the presenter was very friendly. They did a question-and-answer session with some of the audience, and there was a phone-in as well.

"What's your favourite colour?" one caller asked Tara.

"Black," said Tara, at once. She was dressed, as

always, in black jeans and a black T-shirt.

"And what's your favourite hobby?" asked another.

"Writing songs," Tara told him. "It's the best thing in the world."

"Better than being a famous pop star?" asked the presenter.

"Well…" said Tara. "That's fun too!"

They got a huge round of applause when they played "Sky Blue", and then they went back to sit on the studio couch.

After a few more questions, this time from the studio audience, the programme ended with everyone taking part in the custard-pie fight.

"That was great," sighed Tara, at the end of the day. "But you didn't need to rub that custard pie quite so hard into my hair, Ben."

"I just fancied seeing you in something other than black for a change," teased Ben. "The yellow custard-pie hat looked great!"

Back at school, Pop, Lolly and Marmalade wanted to hear all about it, but Charlie was a pain.

"I wouldn't go on such a stupid programme," he told Tara loftily.

Ed laughed. "What a pity," he teased. "I'd love to see you with a big custard pie in the middle of your face!"

"I wish I'd been able to bring one back for you," growled Tara. She knew she shouldn't let Charlie's taunting get to her, but she simply couldn't help it. Somehow, he always managed to get under her skin, no matter how hard she tried to ignore him.

The one thing that helped to calm her down was to work on a song, so Tara made her escape and went to fetch her precious notebook and the old guitar from her room. She tucked herself away in a sunny spot in the school grounds, and went to work.

The newly strung guitar was a real help with the tune. Tara wasn't a great acoustic guitarist, but she knew most of the chords, and could pick out a tune well enough. Soon, she had a new riff developing nicely. At this rate she'd eventually have enough pieces for a whole album!

While it was quiet, she decided to text her father. *Did JJ phone you?* she texted. *I need an acoustic for songwriting...for my birthday maybe? I have fan mail! Miss you,* she added at the end.

She did miss her parents. They were away so much. She knew how much they loved her, but it was still hard. Most of all she missed being with her father, because he was a musician too, and they got on so well.

But Tara was good at coping. When she *did* get to see her father again it would be *great!* In the meantime, her songwriting was going well – so well she hadn't realized how late it was getting. The sun was going down, and she should have been back in her room.

She gathered up her belongings and made her way along the path, thinking about the week ahead. Tomorrow, after school, they could watch themselves appearing on *Monday Madness*. That would be fun! And they had the opening of the local music shop on Friday, but for most of the week there would be normal lessons to go to. With luck she'd have some time to devote to her writing as well. It never took her the whole lunch break to eat her food, and there was a bit of free time in the afternoon before homework had to be done. She could use those times for working on her tunes and lyrics.

Tara was excited by the idea of producing a whole album of her songs. She was sure that Mr. Timms, who ran the school recording studio, would allow her to record them, and she knew Ben, Ed and Danny would help. If she did that, maybe she could send a disc to a music publishing company, or an agent. She'd have to ask Judge Jim about it. He'd know the best places to try. She could imagine how excited she'd feel if she sold a song to a megastar. It would be amazing to hear her song being sung by someone really famous. Or maybe one of her songs might be used to launch the career of a new artist. She'd be a star maker, and have the thrill of seeing her work help someone make it to number one!

Tara was sure she ought to capitalize on her competition win if she could. Now, when people were more likely to know about her, was the perfect time to sell her songs. In fact, in a way, it was a pity they had so many gigs lined up. Not that Tara was resentful. But gigging did take up precious time, which could be spent writing songs. Maybe she was at the beginning of a whole new career!

Tara zipped back to her room, all ready to tell the others what she'd been thinking, but when she got there Chloe was nowhere to be seen, and Pop and Lolly were looking very worried.

6 Disaster!

"Where's Chloe?" asked Tara. "What's the matter with you two?"

"Oh Tara, it's terrible!" said Pop, her eyes as big as saucers. "Chloe's ill."

"Is that all!" said Tara. "The way you and Lolly looked I thought there'd been a real disaster. What's she done? Eaten too much of that cake at tea?"

"No!" said Lolly. "Or at least I don't think so."

"She feels awful," said Pop. "So we took her to sickbay and came back here to tell you."

Tara wrinkled her lip. "So?" she said.

"But aren't you *worried*?" demanded Pop.

"I'm sure she'll be back to her normal self soon,"

said Tara. "I'm sorry if I seem heartless, but what's the problem? Everyone gets sick from time to time."

"But what about your gigs?" said Pop.

Tara stared at her. She hadn't thought about that. "Well...we don't have one for the next few days," she said. "And hopefully she'll be better by Friday."

"But Sister said that there's this horrible flu going around," Pop told her. "And she thinks that Chloe's probably got it. If so, it could easily be a week before she's better."

"Oh, I didn't know that, did I?" snapped Tara, suddenly feeling as worried as Pop and Lolly looked. "Sorry," she added, wishing she had a less prickly nature.

"We wondered if we ought to text the boys," suggested Lolly. "It's too late to go and meet them now."

"That's true," said Tara. "And yes, I suppose we should let them know, just in case we have to think of what to do if she's not well enough for the next gig. It's just the opening of the local music shop extension, but it would be an awful shame to let them down."

"Do you want me to text?" offered Pop.

"No, it's okay. I ought to let them know," said Tara, picking up her phone.

She texted the boys, and soon there were lots of messages flying about between them. The boys were horrified at the possibility of cancelling any gigs, but no one could come up with an alternative. Then Ed had an idea.

Why not ask Pop 'n' Lolly to fill in? he sent.

But no one sings like Chloe, protested Tara.

True, Ed texted back. *But they'd be better than no one.*

Tara told Pop and Lolly what Ed had suggested.

"Well, I'd be willing to learn the song if you want us to," said Lolly at last. "But it wouldn't be the same."

"We sort of know it anyway," said Pop, "because we've heard you play it quite a lot."

"Can you play the tune on your acoustic guitar?" asked Lolly. "We could run through it now if you like."

Tara picked out the tune on the old guitar, and the girls did their best. But they were never going to be as good as Chloe, and they all knew it. By the time Mrs. Pinto came to tell them it was time for bed they had already stopped rehearsing, and were feeling rather disheartened.

"If only we knew for certain when Chloe was going to be well again," said Lolly, as they put their light out.

"You never know," said Pop. "You might not need us."

Tara settled down under her duvet. All they could do was wait, and hope. There was no point in panicking, however long it took Chloe to get well. But it was so frustrating not to know. The twins were never going to sound like Chloe, however hard they tried. Whatever should they do?

In the morning, the remaining band members had a quick meeting with Mrs. Sharkey after breakfast. She advised them to ask Pop and Lolly to learn "Sky Blue". "Sister seems clear now that Chloe *definitely* has flu," she told them. "So she could still be unwell on Friday, when your next gig is. You can't afford to hang on and hope she'll be well in time."

"But the shop might not want Pop and Lolly instead of Chloe," said Ed in a worried voice.

"I'll phone to find out," said Mrs. Sharkey. "Then you'll know where you are, but for now, let's assume you'll be using them, so have a quick rehearsal during morning break to see how you get on."

Afterwards, Tara went to the sickbay to see how Chloe was. Sister O'Flannery wouldn't let her into the room, in case she picked up the flu, but she was allowed to stand in the doorway.

Chloe was really apologetic about being ill, but Tara told her not to worry.

"You can't help being sick," she said.

"Well said," agreed Sister firmly.

"You concentrate on feeling well," said Tara. "The really vital gig is Singing for the World, and I'm sure you'll be fine for that."

"Oh I hope so!" said Chloe, looking very upset. "I couldn't bear it if I had to miss that." She lay back on her pillows and closed her eyes.

"I'm sure you'll be fine by then," smiled Sister. "But

you ought to rest now. Off you go, Tara. Leave my patient in peace."

Back in the dining room Tara discovered that Mrs. Sharkey had already been in touch with the shop.

"They still want us to come," Danny told her. "And they were delighted when Mrs. Sharkey suggested Pop and Lolly as replacement vocalists."

"Well, I suppose Pop and Lolly *are* pretty famous," said Ben. "Which is probably what matters most for things like shop openings."

"Let's meet at the Rock Department at eleven for a quick run-through with them," suggested Ed. "We can work on 'Sky Blue' at lunchtime too."

It was a bit of a scramble, but they managed to run through the song a couple of times at break, and Judge Jim got sandwiches sent over to the Rock Department for lunch, so they could spend all their lunch break there. That saved a lot of time.

Tara certainly couldn't fault the twins' professionalism. They tried really hard with "Sky Blue", and soon got the hang of working with the band. But they struggled to reach some of the notes Chloe sang so easily.

"Chloe took *ages* before she was comfortable singing with a band," Tara told Pop and Lolly. "But you've slotted in really quickly."

"That's probably because we're used to fitting in, and doing what we're told when we're modelling," said Lolly. "But Chloe is still the one you want. Her voice is totally unique. We can't come anywhere near it. And the song is much better suited to her voice than ours."

"It'll be okay," Danny told Tara as they broke up. "Pop and Lolly have been great, stepping in like this, and we still have three days to practise."

"I just hope Chloe only misses this one gig," said Tara. "The song isn't the same without her." Then her phone vibrated, and she tugged it out of her pocket. It was her father calling.

Tara told him all about the drama of Chloe's illness, and he was very sympathetic. "But I want to know about your songwriting," he continued. "It sounds as if you're really getting into it."

"I am!" she said.

"Judge Jim told me you've borrowed an acoustic guitar for now. Can you make do with that until the holidays?" he asked.

"Yes," said Tara, feeling a bit disappointed. Her birthday was before the end of term, and it would have been nice to have had one for that.

"Oh good," said her father. "Only I thought it would be fun to go shopping for a guitar together."

Tara's eyes lit up. "That would be fantastic!" she said. "If you have time."

"I'll *make* time," he said.

After the call, Tara's eyes were shining. It was wonderful to be able to discuss her favourite hobby with her father. And now she had a great shopping trip to look forward to as well. With Pop and Lolly practising hard, the music shop opening on Friday should be okay too. Things were definitely looking up!

7 Another Patient

Although it was a real shame that Chloe couldn't be there, the band enjoyed the shop opening. Mr. Barset, the owner, did all the talking, and his wife cut the ribbon to open the extension. They had asked the band if they would like to use some of the shop instruments to play "Sky Blue". Danny was used to having a drum kit provided for him when he played at gigs, and the others were used to using different amps, but the guitarists had never been offered instruments before today.

"Let's go for it!" said Tara, who had spotted a wicked Fender bass that she fancied trying.

They'd had plenty of time to try the different

instruments before the opening. Ed spied a classic Fender Stratocaster, and was speechless with pleasure when Mr. Barset told him he could play it, while Ben chose a Gibson. It almost felt like Christmas!

They were ready just in time. Friday was always a busy shopping day in the town and, with lots of local children arriving after school, there was quite a crowd.

The band got a loud cheer after they played, and then they had to pose in front of the shop for photographs with the owner and his wife. Afterwards they spent ages signing autographs.

"Those cymbals were seriously good," muttered Danny to Tara, as they waited for Ben to sign a last autograph. "I wish I could take them home with me."

"The bass was good too," said Tara. "I haven't played a Fender before. But I still prefer my Rickenbacker," she added, loyally. "Are you all right?" she asked. "You look awfully pale."

"I'm just feeling a bit chilly," said Danny. "I'll be all

right when we get back indoors."

Tara looked at him worriedly. "It's not cold," she told him. "How can you possibly be chilly?"

The shop had laid on drinks and nibbles, but Tara noticed that Danny hardly ate anything, and by the time they set off home in the minibus he was looking quite feverish.

"Come on," she told him, as soon as they got back. "You have to go and see Sister. You're not well."

Danny was shivering too hard to protest, so Ben rushed off to get his things from their room, while Tara took him up to sickbay.

"Oh no!" said Chloe, when they arrived. She was up and about, and ready to go back to her room, though still feeling a bit wobbly.

"Come on then, Danny," said Sister O'Flannery, kindly. "It looks as if you've got the flu too. Several people have gone down with it now."

"But we have more gigs lined up," said Tara. "And a TV interview."

"Well, we can't help that," said Sister.

"Is he all right?" asked Ben, who had just arrived with Danny's washbag.

"No," said Tara.

"Get Charlie to play instead of me," said Danny, looking worse by the moment. "Don't cancel any of the gigs…" All at once he swayed alarmingly and Sister put her arm around him.

"Come on," she said. "Into bed with you. You're not going to get better standing here."

Ben quickly put the washbag down on the table and exchanged looks with Tara.

"We'd better go," she said.

"I'll come with you," said Chloe. "Sister said I could go back to my own room now."

Halfway down the stairs, Tara suddenly stopped and grabbed Ben's arm. "We can't ask Charlie to fill in for Danny," she told him. "Think how horrible he's been about our success. He'll be *unbearable* if we go now and beg him to bail us out."

"He's not *that* bad," said Ben. "It's just that you let him get to you. And when he finds someone who responds to his taunting he concentrates on them. Do you remember how mean he was to Danny ages ago? But they get on okay now."

"Well of course I'll do what it takes if gigs are being threatened," Tara said. "But I can't help not liking Charlie much, and if he thinks I'll put up with his stupid behaviour he's got another think coming! At least Pop and Lolly did their best, but Charlie will mess about and be difficult. I know he will. *You* know what he's like. It'll be a nightmare."

Tara stomped down the rest of the stairs in a temper. But there was nothing she could do. Danny had been right. Charlie *was* the obvious choice as a stand-in. In spite of everything, he was a good drummer. They would have to ask him.

Tara half wished that *she* could go down with the horrible flu. At least then she wouldn't have to put up with Charlie Owen. But that was silly. She couldn't abandon Wizard Monkey Breath. She wanted the band to do justice to the rest of the gigs and appearances they would make. No doubt Charlie would need to be kept in line, but she was determined that he wouldn't ruin things, however difficult he might be.

Ben gave Ed a call on his mobile phone, and told him to come over to the main building for an emergency meeting.

"It's great to see you back again," Ed told Chloe as soon as he arrived.

"But it's awful Danny's gone down with it now," said Chloe. "He really holds the band together."

Everyone looked glum, but Tara felt the worst of all. In a band, the drummer and bassist had to work closely together, and she wasn't looking forward to doing that with Charlie one bit.

"Will you be able to cope?" Ben asked her anxiously.

"Oh I'll cope," said Tara grimly, determined that Charlie wouldn't get the better of her.

"I expect we'll see him at tea," said Chloe. "Shall we ask him straight away?"

"There's no point waiting," said Tara, gloomily. "Come on. Let's get it over with."

She led the way into the dining room, and spotted

Charlie at a nearby table, chatting with a couple of his friends. He looked startled as almost all the members of Wizard Monkey Breath made their way purposefully towards him.

"What is it?" he asked, looking askance at the way they were all standing over him with their arms folded.

"Charlie Owen," said Tara, determined not to give him the upper hand. "We want a word with you."

8 Charlie Joins the Band

Instead of crowing over their misfortune, Charlie was flabbergasted by what Tara had to say.

"You mean, you actually want me to play with you?" he asked for the second time. "Are you sure?"

"Of course we're sure!" snapped Tara.

"Only until Danny is better again," explained Ben. "It would be great if you could fill in for him while he's sick."

"We have an interview with the local TV station tomorrow," said Chloe. "But we won't be playing, so we won't need you for that. The next gig is in a few days, on Wednesday, and Danny might not be able to play. It took me a week to recover." She looked at

Charlie anxiously. "It's in a big, indoor shopping mall," she told him. "And it's a schools' event. There will be lots of kids there, and we're just appearing to round the whole thing off. Will you be able to learn the song in time?"

Charlie still looked stunned. "Well, yes," he said. "I should think so." He thought for a moment. "There's only one really complicated little bit that Danny put in," he said. "And I think I know how he did it. I'll have a go at it after tea." He looked up at them, and Tara could see that he was genuinely blown away by being asked to help.

"We must have a run-through all together as well," she suggested, feeling a bit more friendly towards him.

"Yes," he agreed straight away. "When do you want to do that?"

"How about we give you half an hour on your own, then we meet in the Rock Department after that?" suggested Ben.

"But my drums are set up in one of the practice rooms in the main building," objected Charlie.

"Yes, but those rooms are too small for all of us," Ed pointed out. "Danny's drums are already set up in the main room in the Rock Department. I'm sure he wouldn't mind you using them, especially as it's an emergency."

Charlie only hesitated for a moment. "Okay then," he agreed.

Tara bit back a grin. Charlie had always poked fun at Danny's drums, and it was true, they weren't anything like as special as Charlie's red sparkle kit. But it looked as if Charlie had decided to go along with almost anything if it meant he could be a temporary member of Wizard Monkey Breath!

"Well!" said Tara, as she and Chloe made their way to their room after tea. "That didn't exactly go as I expected."

"He was *thrilled* to be asked," said Chloe. "So I'm sure he'll be fine. And anyway, Danny's bound to be well again by next weekend. Charlie will only have to play the one gig."

At the run-through, Tara was pleased with Charlie's attitude. He'd obviously worked hard on Danny's part, and although it wasn't perfect, Charlie was a good enough drummer to carry it off. They played "Sky Blue" all the way through a couple of times, and Tara helped him to get the timing right.

"I think it'll be okay," Ed told Charlie. "Your style is different from Danny's, so it'll never sound quite the same, but I can't imagine many people will notice."

"The main thing is for you and Tara to keep us all in time," said Ben. "As long as you two are together, the rest of us will be fine."

It was lucky that the next day was Saturday. The band was able to have a rehearsal in the morning without having to worry about missing lessons. And by the time Judge Jim turned up to take Tara, Chloe, Ed and Ben to the local TV studio, the band was feeling positive about Charlie's contribution.

"How's it going with Charlie?" Judge Jim asked them as they set off.

"Fine!" they chorused.

"And how are you, Chloe?" he said.

"Much better," she told him. "I'll be okay for the gig on Wednesday."

"That's the one in the shopping centre, isn't it?" he asked. "It's always packed with shoppers."

Tara nodded.

"It should be fun," said Ben. "It's a shame Danny's going to miss it."

"But he'll be fine for the others," said Ed. "The festival's coming up next Saturday, and then it's Singing for the World on Sunday. That's the big one!"

Judge Jim smiled. "Yes, it is," he agreed. "It's fantastic you've been invited to play at it. I was involved with the first one, and it was a wonderful experience that I'll never forget. But I don' suppose it'll be the last you'll see of fame," he said. "Except maybe for Tara. I have a feelin' she's more interested in back-room stuff...writin' rather than performin'. That right, Tara?"

Tara smiled. "Could be," she told him. "If I can be successful at writing and selling songs, that'll be what

I want to concentrate on." She waved the slim notebook that went everywhere with her. "This is the most precious thing I own," she told them.

"Even more than your Rickenbacker bass?" asked Ed.

"Yep," she said. "You can always buy a new bass, but if anything happened to this notebook I'd be sunk. It's got all my songs in it, and all the new things I'm working on as well."

"Well, I hope when it comes to me making my first recording I can use one of your songs," said Chloe. "They're really great for my voice."

"I'll see what I can do," said Tara, rifling through the pages of the notebook, mock seriously. "Just get your agent to give me a call!"

Because they'd been on TV before, the interview wasn't at all scary. The local TV company had a regular news programme on a Saturday, and made a habit of talking to local people who had done interesting things.

"I hear there has been some illness in the band," the interviewer said.

"Yes," said Ed. "Danny, our drummer, should be here, but he's not well at the moment."

"So how does that work when you have gigs to do?" asked the interviewer. "It must be a bit of a nightmare."

"Not really," said Ben. "We've got a stand-in drummer until Danny is better. It'll be fine."

The following afternoon, the friends made their way to the Rock Department for another rehearsal with Charlie. After a few minutes, he turned up with several of his friends in tow.

"What are you doing?" said Tara. "We don't want an audience."

Charlie looked very put out. "My mates have come along to watch me play," he told her. "They won't be in the way."

"I don't care," said Tara, getting rather cross. "We've got work to do on 'Sky Blue'. And you need to concentrate, not show off in front of your friends."

"Tara's right," said Ben. "They'll have to leave. Sorry."

Charlie glared at Tara, but she wasn't about to budge.

"Okay, guys," he said to his friends. It was obvious he felt embarrassed and was trying not to show it. "Band stuff. Private. You know how it is. I'll catch you later."

As soon as they'd gone he turned on Tara. "Don't *ever* do that to me again," he hissed.

Tara shrugged. "I won't, so long as you remember not to bring people into rehearsals again," she told him.

"Come on now, you two," said Chloe. "Don't argue."

They did a run-through, but Tara wasn't in a good mood with Charlie, and he seemed determined to be difficult.

"No wonder you didn't want an audience," he sneered, when she uncharacteristically fluffed a couple of notes.

"Everyone makes mistakes from time to time," Chloe told him mildly, but Tara's expression told everyone that she didn't appreciate Charlie's comments.

By the end of the rehearsal, Charlie had succeeded in needling Tara so much she was just about ready to explode, but she held herself in until she and Chloe got back to their boarding house.

"I *knew* it was too good to be true," she told Chloe, Pop and Lolly, before throwing herself onto her bed. "It didn't take long for him to stop being nice and get back to his old self, did it?"

"Well you did embarrass him in front of his friends," Chloe said. "He was bound to take that badly."

"Well he shouldn't have been so stupid," Tara said. "If he's not going to take this seriously he shouldn't be in the band."

"But he's the best alternative you've got to Danny," said Pop. "Isn't he? Surely you can get along together for a few days?"

"Huh!" said Tara. "Thank goodness it *will* only be for a few days. I tell you, as soon as we get back from the gig on Wednesday I'm going straight up to sickbay to demand that Danny comes back, sick or not!"

9 Tara's Problem

True to her word, the minibus had hardly come to a stop back at Rockley Park after the shopping mall gig, when Tara got out and flew up the steps into the main house. As she'd feared, Charlie had managed to make the gig a total misery for her. It seemed he didn't intend to forgive her for making him feel silly in front of his friends, and he was horribly clever at finding the chinks in her armour. In the minibus on the way back to school, he picked at each little unevenness in her playing. He even argued with her about her timing, although she knew it was spot on. And he insisted that her sound was awful, although it was the bad acoustics in the shopping mall that had made the band sound tinny, not anything to do with the way they played. The worst thing was that he managed to make most of his comments out of earshot of everyone else. That made it look as if Tara was totally overreacting.

She arrived at the sickbay rather out of breath, and knocked on the door.

"How's Danny?" she asked Sister O'Flannery. "Is he better? Can I speak to him?"

"Hello, Tara," said Sister. "Come in. You can have a quick word with him as long as you stay by the door. Just in case."

"But he will be back in school again tomorrow, won't he?" she demanded. "He *is* almost better?"

"Unfortunately not," Sister told her. "He's got a terrible cough now, though the doctor has given him some medicine to help it."

"So when *will* he be all right?" asked Tara in horror. "Chloe was better by this stage."

"It's difficult to tell," said Sister, not unkindly. "Not everyone's the same, you know. We'll just have to give it time."

"Will he be okay by Sunday?" Tara asked. That was the day of Singing for the World. Surely he wouldn't miss that?

But Sister O'Flannery shook her head. "I really don't know," she said.

Tara looked in to see Danny lying in bed looking very pale indeed. "Sorry," he said in a quiet voice. "But Charlie played all right today, didn't he?"

"Of course," said Tara. "Don't you worry about that."

Danny looked relieved. "That's all right then," he muttered, and closed his eyes.

Sister shut his door, and Tara followed her to the sickbay entrance. "He will *be* all right, won't he?" she asked, anxiously.

"Of course!" said Sister O'Flannery. "It's just a matter of time."

That was a relief, but Tara went back downstairs feeling totally dejected. She'd coped with Charlie's constant jibes by telling herself that he'd be out of the band by the end of the day, but now she could see that she was going have to put up with him for a bit longer.

It's impossible! she told herself. *He'll drive me absolutely mad. I'm sure he's trying to get me so wound up I'll refuse to play, and then he'll bring in one of his bass-playing friends to make me feel completely useless!*

That was a terrible thought. Tara was absolutely determined that she wouldn't let that happen. But how would she cope? Charlie made her so furious with him she didn't know if she was coming or going.

The band had to go to the gig at the three-day festival some way from Rockley Park on Saturday. On Thursday and Friday, Tara and Chloe went to find out how Danny was, but by Friday, although he was making progress, it was obvious he wasn't going to be well enough to play the following day.

Tara had been looking forward to the festival, but now she was dreading the journey. Spending three hours in the minibus listening to Charlie making snide comments about her wasn't exactly her idea of a good time. Besides, she had an idea for some new lyrics, but was sure he wouldn't leave her in peace, like the others did, when she was busy writing.

Ed and Ben always sat together on the bus, and Chloe tended to alternate between sitting with Danny or Tara, but of course Danny was still in sickbay, so Chloe and Tara shared a seat. That left Charlie. He sat opposite the boys, and they all chatted together. Tara heaved a sigh of relief. Maybe the journey wouldn't be so bad after all. For a while, she and Chloe chatted too, and then Tara pulled out her notebook.

"Do you mind if I do some work?" she asked Chloe.

"Not at all," said Chloe, with a smile. "Are you going to be working on my first hit record?"

"You never know!" grinned Tara.

"I'll go and talk to the others," Chloe said, and moved up a couple of seats to chat to the boys.

For a while Tara was left in peace. As the time passed, she got on really well with the new lyrics. She was so absorbed, she didn't notice that Charlie had moved opposite her. The first couple of bits of screwed-up paper he threw at her fell short, and Tara was none the wiser, but then one hit her on the head and she looked up.

"Got you!" Charlie flicked another bit of paper at her and it hit her in the face.

Tara frowned. "Cut it out," she told him grumpily, annoyed to have been distracted.

"What are you doing then?" he asked.

"Nothing," she said, trying to shield the notebook from his prying eyes.

"If it was nothing you wouldn't be hiding the book," he told her. "What is it? A love letter?" He sniggered, and Tara glowered at him.

"They're song lyrics," she told him. "And you're stopping me from working on them."

"Ooo! Get you!" he teased. "Let's have a look. Go on. Give us all a laugh." He made a grab for the book and Tara shouted at him.

"Get off, Charlie!"

Judge Jim, who was driving, heard the argument.

"What's goin' on?" he called over his shoulder.

"Charlie's trying to take my notebook!" Tara told him.

"It was just a joke," said Charlie.

"Go back to your place, Charlie," said Judge Jim. "And behave yourselves, everyone. If I'd realized you needed lookin' after like little kids, I'd have brought another teacher with me."

Charlie sneered at Tara before moving back to sit with the boys. "Songwriting!" he scoffed.

Tara folded her arms, trembling with fury. How dare he try to grab her notebook! And now he'd totally ruined her train of thought. She stuffed the notebook into her back pocket and sat glaring out at the scenery.

As soon as they got to the festival they unloaded their instruments and started a soundcheck. They were performing in the middle day of the festival, so everything was in full swing. They did their soundcheck at the smaller of the two stages, where they were booked to perform. Then they all decided to go and get some food from one of the many stalls dotted around.

"I fancy one of those tortilla wraps," Tara said to Chloe. "Coming?"

"Sounds good," said Chloe. "What about you, Ed?

Charlie! What are you doing?"

Charlie had sneakily pulled the notebook out of Tara's pocket and was flicking through the pages.

"Give that back, Charlie Owen!" screamed Tara. She grabbed at the book, but Charlie held it up high, out of her reach.

"Come on, Charlie, stop it," said Ben.

Charlie turned his back on Tara and looked inside the notebook. "*Every day I'm so alone*," he read out in a silly voice.

"Charlie!" Tara was practically in tears.

"Give it back," said Ed, coldly.

Ben jumped up and managed to snatch it out of Charlie's hand.

"Careful!" screamed Tara.

Ben handed the book over and Tara tried to smooth out the crumpled pages. "You *idiot*," she told Charlie, her voice trembling. "How *dare* you do that? Don't you touch my things *ever* again." She looked at Ben gratefully. "Thanks," she muttered. She started to put the book into her back pocket again but then changed her mind. Instead, she carefully rolled it up and pushed it into the front pocket of her jeans. It stuck out rather a lot, but at least it would be safer from Charlie.

"What's goin' on?" asked Judge Jim, appearing with a cardboard plate of Cajun chicken. "You all right, Tara?" he added, noticing the furious expression on her face.

"I am now," she told him, icily.

"Well, get a move on and find some food," he advised them all. "You ought to be backstage in half an hour, ready for your slot at two thirty."

By the time they were waiting to go onstage, Tara had come to an uneasy truce with Charlie. There was no way she was ready to forgive him for taking her notebook. It had been humiliating for her to realize that, because he was so much taller and stronger than her, she might never have got it back if Ben hadn't grabbed it for her. Thank goodness the others had been there. She was very grateful to Ben for retrieving it.

Tara had decided that she had to be professional about Charlie. She would speak to him when she had to, and be helpful as far as anything to do with their performance was concerned. But that was as far as she would go. She adjusted the shoulder strap of her Rickenbacker and tapped the top of her notebook. Yes. It was still safe. Good.

Ben gave her a grin. Tara could hear their names being announced. And then they were on!

In spite of their troubles, it was a good performance. The music took them over and arguments were forgotten, as Chloe's voice soared with the lyrics Tara had written for "Sky Blue". Tara ignored Charlie. She and Danny had a habit of keeping in touch with the occasional glance when they performed, but she didn't bother to look at Charlie. He was doing all right, and that was all that mattered.

Afterwards, Tara and the boys slid their guitars into their cases and waited for Judge Jim to meet them backstage.

"Well done," he told them as soon as they met. "You went down a storm! And I overheard someone say that you were the best lookin' bassist he'd seen for a while, Tara."

Tara found herself blushing. "It's the music that matters," she growled, to cover her embarrassment, but all the same, it was very nice to have been paid a compliment.

On the way home, Chloe and Tara sat together again, and chatted happily about the gig. Tara's steely tactic of ignoring Charlie seemed to be having some effect, and he left her alone for a change.

"Only one more gig on our itinerary," sighed Chloe, when they were almost home. "And it's tomorrow! I wonder if there will be any more? I do hope Danny is okay for it."

"Me too," agreed Tara. "Singing for the World is *so* important."

"It'll be terribly sad for him if he can't do it," said Chloe. "But you told me he was feeling better when you saw him yesterday."

"Yes," said Tara. "But Sister said he still needed a bit of time to build up his energy. Hopefully he's done that today."

Chloe sighed. "The audience will be massive. A

whole football stadium full of people! And there'll be worldwide TV coverage as well. I can't *believe* we're going to be part of it."

"And afterwards we'll just be students again," said Tara. "And have to concentrate on catching up on the lessons we've missed."

"We'll never *just* be students," objected Chloe. "We'll always be the students who won the International Battle of the Bands competition in Italy. No one can take that away from us."

"That's true," smiled Tara. "I reckon we'll always be proud of that."

Chloe and Charlie didn't have instruments to put away, so it was Tara and the boys who accompanied Judge Jim to the Rock Department and unloaded.

"What are you up to this evening?" asked Ed, when they'd finished.

"I'm going to relax in front of the TV for a change," said Ben. "How about you, Tara? Are you going to relax, or will you be songwriting again?"

Tara grinned. "I might do a bit more," she agreed, "now Charlie's out of the way." She tapped her pocket where the notebook should be and her face grew pale.

"My notebook!" She felt in all her pockets and started to panic. "It's gone!"

10 Missing

"Your notebook can't have gone," said Ben. "I saw you put it in your pocket, and Charlie hasn't been anywhere near you since before the gig."

"It m-must have fallen out," stammered Tara in a horrified voice. "This pocket isn't as deep as the back one, which is why I usually keep the notebook there. I only swapped pockets so it was safe from Charlie."

"Well, don't panic," said Ed. "I bet it fell out when you got into the minibus. I'll get the key and we can look."

Within a couple of minutes he'd fetched the key, and all three of them frantically searched the minibus.

"It's not here!" said Tara, in a wavering voice, when Judge Jim came out to see how they were getting on.

"It must have gone while we were at the festival! We've got to go back and find it!"

Judge Jim looked serious. "We can't do that," he told her. "It's too far away. I'll phone the organizers. But don't hold out a lot of hope, Tara. There's such a lot of litter at a festival. Chances are it'll have been cleared away by the stewards and put in a rubbish bin by now. What colour was the notebook? Did it have your name in it?"

"Blue," said Tara, miserably. "And yes, my name was in it. I'd rolled it up to put it in my pocket," she added, dolefully. "So I'm afraid it might not look very important to litter pickers."

"Okay. I'll go and ring them now," said Judge Jim.

"Thanks," sniffed Tara, having difficulty in keeping back the tears. Losing her precious notebook was a *huge* disaster.

"Look, never mind," said Ed, awkwardly, when Judge Jim had gone. "Come and have some tea. There's still time."

"I can't," said Tara, frantically. "I have to write down

all the songs I can remember before I forget them. I need paper…and a pen." She was ignoring the tears that were trickling down her cheeks, and feeling in her pockets for her pen.

"Here," Ben offered her a piece of paper and a stub of pencil. "Shall I get you some more from indoors?"

"No…no," she said. "Thanks. I must just go and…" She turned and walked away without another word.

Tara was in such a state she didn't know what she was doing. Her mind flitted from one song to another, and one new snatch of a tune to a riff she'd created months ago. They were all jostling in her mind, all desperate not to be forgotten, and yet she was so agitated she didn't know where to begin. She couldn't sit down and concentrate, so she just kept walking, trying to hold everything in her head, desperate not to forget one note or one word. It was all such a jumble, she didn't even know where she was heading.

By the time she came to her senses she was most of the way down Rockley Park's long drive. For a few mad moments she considered carrying on walking, out of the school and down the road. She could get a bus to London. She could stay with her father, or in a hotel, if he was away. She wouldn't tell anyone where she was. She couldn't face anyone. She hardly dare speak to anyone until she'd written everything down again, but at the same time she didn't know where to start.

For a few minutes she stood in the middle of the drive, too frantic and shaky to do anything. Then she made herself move away, into the shade of a large chestnut tree. She could sit there and write all her songs down before she forgot them.

She tried to make a start, but her hand was trembling so much she could scarcely hold the pencil. When it touched the paper, all the words seemed to disappear from her mind. And as soon as she did get one line down, the next escaped her. She was terrified she would lose her wonderful tunes as well.

It was a warm evening, but Tara felt cold. She rolled onto her front and buried her head in her arms. She couldn't cry. She was past tears. All she could feel was cold misery.

Time passed. Several vehicles came and went. Tea was over, and it was long past time to go in. The sun's rays lengthened and fell on the small figure dressed in black, lying face down under the tree.

Eventually a vehicle came slowly down the drive from the direction of the school. It drove past, and then backed up and stopped opposite the still figure. The engine died. A door opened and clicked quietly closed again.

Judge Jim narrowed his eyes. To begin with he hadn't been sure, but now he'd got out of his car he could see that the dark patch on the grass was indeed Tara. If it hadn't been for the sun falling on her, he would probably have missed her. Everyone else had. He went over to make sure she was all right.

Tara realized that someone was standing beside her, but she couldn't bring herself to acknowledge them. Whoever it was, she didn't want to speak to them. But Judge Jim's voice was so warm and comforting that she found she was listening to what he had to say.

"Reckon you and I should talk awhile," he said,

calmly. He paused before continuing into the silence. "It sure is sweet out here under the trees. That sun eases my poor old bones, but it's tricky for me to sit on the grass. If I get down I don' know if I can get up again!" He paused. "Still. Reckon I'll give it a go."

Judge Jim was more than a teacher to Tara. He and her father were friends, and Tara trusted him more than anyone. His deep, rich voice sounded caring. Slowly she turned her head towards him. All she could see was the knee of his scruffy jeans and his stick, lying on the short grass. Tears started to fall silently from Tara's eyes.

Judge Jim didn't mention the tears, but kept up his slow, comfortable, one-sided conversation with her. Eventually she turned her face away from him again and wiped her eyes on her T-shirt. She sat up slowly and looked at him, feeling fragile but a bit more herself. He stopped mid-sentence and looked at her. She could see real concern in his brown eyes.

"You shouldn't be sitting here," she told him, in a rough voice.

"So are you gonna help me up?" he asked.

Tara nodded and got unsteadily to her feet. She felt about a million years old and hollow inside. The sun had gone from their patch of grass, and a breeze had sprung up. She picked up his stick and held out her hand to pull him up. He smiled. "I think I'd better get half up first," he told her. "Or I'm likely to pull you over."

Just then his phone rang and he answered it. "Yes," he said, quietly. "Havin' a talk. Fine." He put the phone away and they concentrated on getting him back on his feet. With the help of the tree and Tara, Judge Jim pulled himself upright and took the stick. They walked slowly over to his car and got in.

"So," he said. "When there's a crisis, the best thing is to talk it through."

For a while there was silence in the car, and this time Judge Jim didn't seem inclined to speak. Tara traced her finger down a mark on her jeans. Then she stared out through the windscreen at the school gates and the road ahead.

"You'll think I'm stupid," she said, eventually. "I should have made copies of my songs."

"Easy to say with hindsight," he replied. "And no, Tara, I don't think you're stupid at all. I understand what it's like for an artist to lose her work. It hurts deep down."

Tara nodded. He was so right. There was a pain in her heart.

Slowly she started to talk. She told him about Charlie, and how he'd made her life miserable. She told him how she'd tried to ignore him but how she got furious with him, in spite of her efforts. Then she explained about how he'd taken her notebook, and how she'd transferred it to a front pocket, in the hope of keeping it safe from him.

"But I didn't keep it safe, did I?" she said, her voice shaking. "And now it's gone. All my songs have gone." She stared through the windscreen at the dusky light, and it really did feel as if she'd lost everything.

Judge Jim sat quietly for a few minutes. Then he started his car and put it into gear.

"Don' suppose you've eaten," he said. "Fancy a pizza?"

It seemed such an odd thing to say that it jolted Tara out of her introspection.

"But I should have had tea in the dining room," she told him. "And it must almost be time for bed and…" Her voice trailed away. She was too exhausted to think properly.

"And so you need some food," said Judge Jim. "And so do I. Don't you worry about school. They know you're with me."

He drove to the gates and pulled out into the road. "You can't solve problems on an empty stomach," he told her, as they headed into town. "I don' care what anyone says."

He was right. By the time they were tucking into two enormous pizzas, Tara was feeling a lot more positive. They'd borrowed a pad from the manager of the restaurant, and Tara was making a start at reconstructing her songs. It wasn't easy, and she feared that she'd lost some good things for ever, but with Judge Jim helping to keep her calm, she was remembering more than she had expected.

"What next?" said Judge Jim, through a mouthful of pepperoni.

Tara looked up from the pad. "Three of the oldest songs have been recorded by Mr. Timms," she told him. "So I don't need to worry about those. That includes 'Sky Blue', of course," she added, looking at her list.

"Two I can remember pretty well, and so will Ben and Ed because we've played them together a few times." She sighed. "I can't remember all the lyrics though, and there are another three I was working on recently. It's weird. They're the ones I'm having most difficulty with, especially the song I was working on this morning in the minibus…before Charlie snatched the notebook." She bit her lip, determined not to get upset again.

"And how do you feel about playin' with Charlie again tomorrow?" asked Judge Jim quietly.

Tara looked at the teacher in surprise. She'd been so upset at the loss of her notebook she'd forgotten that the biggest gig of her life was tomorrow.

"Well I may not have to," she reminded him. "Danny might be okay. But if he's not..." She tried to be fair. After all, it might have been Charlie's fault that she moved the notebook, but she couldn't totally blame him for her losing it. All the same, if she never saw Charlie Owen again it would be too soon.

"I don't know. I can't *bear* him. He's such an idiot. But..." She paused. "The gig. Singing for the World is the important one. Not because it's so big...but because of raising money for charity. Not that *he'll* see it like that," she burst out. "I bet if he has to play he'll start going on about how clever he is and what a big shot he is because he's performed at it, when he'd only be there because poor Danny was ill."

"Tara. If you really can't stand playin' with him I could ask Danny's drum teacher if he'd stand in for this one gig."

Tara stared at Judge Jim. For a moment she was tempted to accept the offer. But then she thought about how it would look, with all the band members being kids, apart from one adult helping them along, as if they couldn't do it themselves. No. She couldn't let that happen. Charlie might be an idiot, but he could play. If she brought an adult in at this late stage she'd have let the band down. It would be different if *Charlie* let the band down, but Tara couldn't do that.

"It's all right," she told Judge Jim, slowly. "If it has to be Charlie I'll cope somehow. Danny chose him, and he made the right decision. If it can't be Danny, I'm afraid it has to be Charlie."

Judge Jim smiled. "Tara, you have true grit," he said. "And you're a real professional. I admire you." There was silence for a moment. "D'you want some of that stuff they call ice cream in this place?" he asked her.

Tara shook her head. She felt very weary.

"C'mon then," said Judge Jim. "Let's get you back."

They didn't speak much on the way home, but the silence was comfortable. When they arrived outside the boarding house, Tara did something she rarely did to anyone. She gave Judge Jim a hug. "Thank you for helping," she said. "You took how I feel about my songs seriously...and that's brilliant." For a moment she was almost in tears again, and she struggled not to let them fall. "I don't want to let the band down," she said.

"Well then." Judge Jim switched off the engine. "You know, Tara, this would be Charlie's really big chance to shine. He's always been so overshadowed by Danny before. So if he *does* have to perform tomorrow, you'll have done a really kind thing in letting him. Danny is pure class. He'll be there another time. But Charlie, well, he's a great drummer, but who knows?"

Tara opened the car door and slipped out. She closed the door again and leaned in through the open window. "Fair enough," she said. "But I hope Danny makes it. I'd rather have him play than Charlie *any* day."

11 A Challenge for Tara

Early the next morning, Tara and Chloe went straight up to sickbay to see how Danny was. He was sitting up in bed eating a bowl of cereal, and looked a lot better.

"Hi!" said Tara, feeling very pleased. But Danny had bad news for them.

"I'm sorry," he said, putting his spoon down with a clink. "There's no way I can play today. When I get out of bed I've got no energy. And my arms feel so heavy. I think I'd have enough trouble getting onto the stage, let alone drumming."

"But it's Singing for the World!" said Tara.

Danny nodded. "I know," he said. "And I'm gutted to be missing it," he told them. "But I'd be no use to you.

Honestly. I've got no strength at all."

He looked so sad that Tara felt awful for him. "You'll perform there in the future. I'm sure you will," she told him firmly, remembering what Judge Jim had said.

"That's right," agreed Chloe.

Danny smiled at them. "Thanks," he said. "I hope so. Anyway, good luck today. Tell Charlie I'll be watching on TV, so I'll know if he lets the band down. But I'm sure he'll do his best."

"We'd better go," said Chloe. "We're going to have a quick run-through before we set off."

"Okay."

Tara looked at Danny. "Get well soon," she told him. "We miss you."

Wizard Monkey Breath met at the Rock Department for their final, brief rehearsal. Charlie settled himself quietly onto Danny's drum stool without saying anything to Tara, and Tara stayed strictly professional. When his timing was a little slow she made them go back over the song again until he got it right, but she restrained herself from making any comments, and so did he. It wasn't exactly the best atmosphere for a successful band, but it would have to do.

Then, with Judge Jim at the wheel, they set off for the drive to London. Tara and Chloe sat together, right behind Ed and Ben. Tara was determined Charlie should have no opportunity to make any more snide comments out of everyone else's hearing. And although she missed her songwriting, she didn't attempt to do any. She hadn't had one good idea since she'd lost her notebook. Charlie had brought a magazine with him, and he spent the entire journey reading and listening to his MP3 player.

When they got to the football stadium where the gig was taking place, Judge Jim stopped the minibus at the performers' entrance and showed his pass. They were waved through, and parked with loads of other vehicles. Tara hung the pass Judge Jim had given her around her neck and the others did the same. The bright green card stood out against her black T-shirt.

Until Danny had fallen ill, the band had planned on

wearing their special competition clothes for this gig, but Charlie was too big for Danny's blue top and specially dyed, matching jeans. In spite of that they had decided Chloe ought to wear her wonderful white, feathered dress, and so she headed towards the changing area to hang it up, with Tara for company.

"Don't get lost," called Charlie. "I know what you girls are like."

Tara turned to make a scathing response but Chloe caught her arm.

"Don't," she begged. "We have to get through the soundcheck and then perform. We want to be at our best, not arguing."

Tara took a deep breath. "You're right," she agreed. "And he's not worth it."

By the time the girls came back, the engineers were ready for the band to go up for their soundcheck. So Tara and the others climbed the steep steps up onto the back of the stage and out in front of the stacks of amps, past swathes of black power cables taped down so no one would trip over them.

When Tara looked out at the empty space where the audience would be, she gasped. They'd played open-air gigs before, but nothing like as huge as this one. The enormous stadium field was surrounded by stands, large enough to hold thousands of people. Would the audience really fill the grassy space as well? It made her heart swell with emotion.

"This is *unbelievable*," Ben said to Tara in a shaky voice. "Are you scared?"

"We'd be mad not to be a *bit* scared," she replied.

"Look at Charlie," he said, nudging her elbow.

Charlie was standing by the expensive drum kit that was already set up. It was raised up really high, on a huge platform, so Charlie wouldn't be hidden behind the other band members, as drummers usually are. He'd be up there, in full view of everyone, including the cameras. He was standing looking at it, his drumsticks dangling in his limp hand, and his mouth open.

Ed laughed. "At last!" he said. "Something has

rendered him speechless."

"He must be used to seeing set-ups like this, though," said Tara. "After all, his father is a rock drummer, isn't he? And he's been to gigs with him."

"But it's a bit different when you actually have to perform," said Ben. "He looks as if it's just hit him that he's really going to have to come out here and play...right up there!"

"Good!" said Tara. "Maybe he'll be so busy thinking that he'll forget about messing around. We want this to be the best gig ever. We want all those people watching on their TVs to donate *huge* amounts of money when we come on. And we want to make Danny proud."

"Don't fall!" Ed called out to Charlie, who was making his way up the steep steps that led to the drum kit. But Charlie didn't seem to have heard.

Over the next few minutes the sound engineer set the levels separately for each instrument and Chloe's voice. Then he asked them to run through the whole song, together.

"Okay," he told them, when they'd finished. "You're done."

They made their way backstage again. It was a large, tented area, with lots of space for chilling out, eating at the mobile canteen, and meeting people.

"I keep seeing people I recognize," said Chloe, as yet another famous person wandered past.

Judge Jim knew loads of people. It was awesome having so many famous faces coming up to say hello. Judge Jim made a point of introducing them all, which was a real thrill for Tara and the others.

They made their way slowly to the canteen, and queued up for drinks and something to eat. Then they found a quiet corner to sit and eat their lunch, while they watched all the famous faces nearby.

"Isn't that the comedian who has a TV programme on Thursdays?" said Ed, pointing to a tall man on their right.

"Yes!" said Chloe. "What's he doing here?"

"I expect he'll be doing some of the introductions and fill-ins between acts," said Tara.

"Oh. Look who's over there!" It was Sebastian Walters, a famous TV chat-show host. "He's coming over!" said Chloe.

"Hi there, kids!" Sebastian was wearing a dark purple suit, shiny shoes and his trademark hairstyle was unruly, as ever. "How's it going? Excited?" he asked. "I'll be introducing you this afternoon, so I thought I'd better find out a bit about you."

He was very easy to talk to. "Who wrote the song?" he asked, almost straight away.

"Tara," said Chloe at once. "She's a brilliant songwriter!"

"Really?" Sebastian looked impressed. "I do admire people who can write stuff," he told her. "I wish I could. So how do you do it?"

"Well, I used to carry a notebook around with me," Tara told him awkwardly. "But I lost it recently, and haven't had any good ideas since then."

"Oh no!" Sebastian looked appalled. "That's terrible!"

After finding out a little bit about each of them in turn he got up to go. "Good luck this afternoon," he said.

"You're the youngest band we've ever had here, so I'm going to make a big thing of it. I reckon we can get loads of donations with you appearing. People always like to see kids doing their bit!"

"Will you folks be okay if I go over an' speak to a friend?" asked Judge Jim. "I'll just be over there." He pointed to the other side of the Relax Zone, where several people were deep in conversation.

"We'll be fine," Tara told him. "Really."

"Okay then." Judge Jim looked pleased. "I won' be long. Don' wander out of this area. The loos are over there. You can get more to eat if you want, and you're not on for another hour and a half. Just relax. And if you want me, come over. Okay?"

"It's fine," said Chloe.

For a few minutes they chatted together. It was so cool to be amongst all these celebrities. And Charlie wasn't bragging any more, which was nice. In fact he wasn't saying much at all.

"You've gone very quiet, Charlie," said Ben. "Are you all right?"

"There's nothing worth saying," snapped Charlie.

"Sorry!" said Ben.

The others looked at Charlie.

"Are you sure you're all right?" asked Ed.

"You're not coming down with that bug, are you?" said Chloe.

Charlie got up. "You're as bad as Sebastian Walters with all your questions," he told them, crossly. "Just shut up asking me, will you!"

He stormed off in the direction of the loos.

"Well!" Ed looked angry.

Chloe sighed. "I didn't mean to annoy him," she said. "But he's in an awful mood all of a sudden."

"Perhaps he wanted Sebastian to ask *him* more, instead of concentrating on your songwriting, Tara," suggested Ben. "It would be just typical of Charlie."

"Well I hope he'll stay away from us for a while," said Tara. "At least until he cools down. I don't want negative vibes around me. I want us to concentrate on being the best we can this afternoon."

"Too right!" said Ed.

But after an hour, Charlie still hadn't reappeared, and everyone was beginning to feel slightly anxious.

"Where *is* he?" fumed Tara. "He told *us* not to get lost and now *he's* gone missing. I'll *kill* him if he lets us down."

12 Singing for the World

"It won't be long until we're on," Chloe fretted. "I hope Charlie comes back soon."

"But all the acts get a fifteen-minute warning in here, don't they?" Ed reminded her. "He'll hear that."

"I suppose so," said Chloe.

All the same, when Judge Jim came back, and there was still no sign of Charlie, even he looked a little anxious. "Are you sure he didn't go out of the backstage area?" he asked.

"I'm not *sure*," said Ben. "But I think we'd have noticed if he had. We're near the exit here."

"But it's awfully crowded," Chloe pointed out. "He might have sneaked past."

"Well we've got a good half an hour until you're on," said Judge Jim, looking at his watch. "Let's have a look around and see if we can see him. Stay backstage though, and meet back here in five minutes. Okay?"

Tara headed off in the direction of the loos, and Judge Jim went to the entrance to speak to one of the security people.

Tara was sure one of the boys must have gone into the loo to look for Charlie, but she wanted to have a look around the back. The performers' area was divided off from the rest of the stadium ground by canvas walls. There were lots of areas with easy chairs provided, but they were pretty crowded, and Tara wondered if Charlie had found a more private place to chill out. He was too big-headed to want the band to see him mooching about on his own, although he'd complained earlier that not many of his dad's friends were there. Tara could imagine him sneaking off somewhere on his own and then turning up just before their slot, boasting of all the famous friends he'd been making. It would be just like him.

She walked almost all round the Relax Zone without success, and then she got to the backstage area, where bands were called to wait just before they went on. From here she could see a maze of cables disappearing under the stage. She bent down to get a better look. There were boxes, cables, pieces of timber and all sorts of other things lying in the flattened grass. And then she saw what looked very like Charlie's trainer, sticking out from behind a large box.

"Charlie?" she called, but there was no answer. She stood up and folded her arms in annoyance. What on earth was he doing in there? Trust him to go somewhere really stupid.

Tara glanced around, but none of the others was in sight to help, so she ducked down and crept under the stage. The space was almost high enough to stand up in, but not quite. She manoeuvred her way between the struts supporting the stage until she got to the box Charlie was hiding behind. She was ready to give him a good telling-off. What did he think he was doing? Did he think he was being professional? Even really famous people were expected to turn up on time for their slots. His behaviour was threatening to screw up this gig. How could he be so stupid?

But as Tara got to the box she stopped dead. All her angry words vanished. She stared down at Charlie. At first, she wondered if he was asleep, but his eyes were open, and they looked like the eyes of a frightened rabbit caught in the headlights of an oncoming car. He was curled up, clutching his drumsticks to his chest, and he looked so unlike his usual, bragging self that she was shocked. She had to do something. But what?

Tara kneeled down beside Charlie and reached out an uncertain hand. "Charlie?" She touched his sleeve and he jumped, as if she'd given him an electric shock. He sat up hurriedly and hugged his knees, not looking at her.

"I can't play," he told her, in a monotone.

"What?"

"I can't play," he repeated. "I just can't. I didn't have enough rehearsal time. It's not my fault I can't do it."

"But…"

She looked at Charlie. He had stage fright. That must be what it was. The great boaster was a gibbering idiot at the thought of going onstage. The hugeness of this gig must have freaked him out. She remembered his expression when he'd seen where he was going to be, stuck up high above everyone else, in full view. Stage fright. It could hit the most unlikely people. But they didn't have time for this. Charlie *had* to go on. Tara couldn't help Charlie. She didn't like him enough to be sympathetic. She'd have to fetch Judge Jim. He'd know what to do.

She started to get up. Charlie stared at her with frightened eyes. "Where are you going?"

"To…" Then she thought again. How would Judge Jim ever get in here, with his bad leg? It would be impossible.

She looked at Charlie's vulnerable face, and remembered what Judge Jim had said about him. This was his really big chance. For the first time he wouldn't be overshadowed by Danny. Danny's misfortune would be his opportunity. And he was about to throw it all away. Surely, if she could, she ought to help him through it? She didn't want to. After the trouble he'd caused her, it was the last thing she felt like doing. But if she didn't talk him round he'd stay here, in a total funk, and Wizard Monkey Breath would let everyone down.

"Charlie." She kneeled back down beside him. "Listen to me."

It was almost time for the band to go on when Tara and Charlie appeared, arm in arm. The others stared at them in surprise.

"Sorry. Sorry!" said Tara, brightly, brushing off all the recriminations. "We got talking and forgot about the time. But it's okay. We're just being given the last call now!"

"Honestly, Tara. Sometimes I could *kill* you," said Chloe as they scrambled to take their places. She had changed into her beautiful, white, feathered dress, but looked really agitated. "What's going on? My breathing's all wrong now because I was in a panic about you not turning up."

"I have *never* not turned up in time," Tara told her in

a steely voice. "Stop wasting time being cross and do some breathing exercises while we wait for this band to finish."

Judge Jim caught Tara's arm and she had to let go of Charlie. She watched anxiously as he followed the others, then she faced Judge Jim. "Sorry," she said, before he could speak.

"What happened?" he asked her.

"Charlie got stage fright," she muttered.

"Is he okay now?" Judge Jim asked.

"I hope so," said Tara. "Because there's no time to do anything about it."

The band waited down behind the stage. This was the worst time for nerves, and Tara edged her way forwards until she was standing close to Charlie. She knew how fragile his confidence was. She had talked him into being brave, but she didn't know if his courage would hold.

They all stood in silence while Sebastian Walters told a couple of jokes to the audience, and then introduced them. He was leaving the stage as they made their way to the front. He gave Tara a thumbs up and grinned. Tara hung back to watch Charlie take his seat behind the drum kit. He looked down at her with pale and frightened eyes. She nodded at him, trying to look confident, but really she was almost as freaked out as he was. She'd never been onstage with someone with real stage fright before. And the rest of the band didn't know anything about it. What would they do if Charlie couldn't play? Tara took her place and plugged in with shaking hands.

Ben nodded at Charlie to count them in but nothing happened. Tara's heart began to thump. Ben nodded at the drummer again and Tara held her breath. But no sound came from the drums. Now the boys and Chloe were all looking at each other, and Charlie, in bewilderment.

The audience hadn't realized anything was wrong yet, but they very soon would, when the band failed to begin their song.

Tara's mind raced. Charlie had told her that having to start them off was one thing that frightened him, because there were so many thousands of people to get it wrong in front of.

Charlie was too high up for Ed to go over and speak to him easily, but he was staring at the drummer and looking puzzled. Charlie was avoiding everyone by looking down at his bass pedal, as if there might be something wrong with it. But Tara was sure he was frozen with fear. She had to do something, and fast. But what?

In desperation she started to play the bass part of "Sky Blue". The others would kill her for hijacking the beginning of the song, but what else could she do? She played a few notes of a hastily made-up introduction, and went into the verse. If she could catch Charlie's eye, maybe she could get him to come in after she'd played the verse through once – not that it sounded like much, with only Tara playing.

To begin with, absolutely no one joined in. She was left to play more of the bass line of the song on her own, not knowing what would happen next. Chloe had already glared at her, and Tara could feel Ed and Ben's hostility from across the stage. But then, to her utter relief, Ben joined in, playing the tune on top of her bass. That sounded better; she could relax a little. Then Ed came in as well. Tara gave a shaky sigh. Obviously they had no idea what was going on, but at least they were following where she was leading.

They played the first verse of "Sky Blue", and Chloe sang it for her. It actually sounded rather nice without drums for a change, but it wasn't right. Tara thought of Danny watching, as bewildered as the rest of them. She had to get Charlie to play, but how?

As soon as the verse ended, Tara went into the bridge. She couldn't play the verse through again. If she did, poor Chloe would be totally lost. But Charlie still wasn't coming in. So while they played the bridge, Tara moved across the stage to speak to Ben.

"What are you doing?" he hissed at her.

"Go to the beginning again in a minute," she told him. "Try to make it sound as if we meant it like this."

Ben scowled at her, but there wasn't a lot he could do. Tara had left him now, and was heading towards the drums. As the bridge ended, she yelled up at Charlie, as loudly as she could, against the speakers' high volume. She used all her pent-up frustration and anger with him, and bellowed it out to break through his trance.

"CHARLIE!"

Charlie jumped, and Tara waved her fist at him. "GO FOR IT!"

They were coming round to the next verse, and to her huge relief, Charlie lifted his sticks and started to play. To begin with it was faltering, but after a couple of bars he was away.

And then Charlie *did* go for it, gaining in confidence all the while, until he was giving a storming performance. As the song came to an end, applause rang out and the band members bowed. Sebastian Walters came running back onstage and added his applause to that of the enormous audience.

Chloe put her microphone back on its stand and joined the others, who were already moving offstage.

"Don't go. Don't go!" said Sebastian. He brought

them back and urged the audience to cheer again.

"I want all of you at home to dig deep and phone in with your credit card numbers, now! These kids have played their hearts out for you today, and if they can do their bit, you can do yours, too. So get on the phone and call now. Okay. Let's hear it one more time for Wizard Monkey Breath!"

As Tara turned to follow the others offstage, he caught her arm. "Here," he said. "Thought you might like this. Take care now."

"You shouldn't have done that," fumed Ed, as they climbed down from the stage. "Why did you start off the song?" He, Ben and Chloe were angry and very confused. But Charlie was looking at Tara and grinning all over his face.

"I did it!" he yelled, triumphantly. "I did it!"

"Well done for coping when Tara went walkabout with the song," said Ed. "We didn't have a clue what she was up to. She should have waited for you to start us off, even though you were rather slow. Was there something wrong with your drum pedal?"

Tara exchanged glances with Charlie. The others didn't seem to have realized that it was Charlie who had messed up, not her. She waited for him to own up that he'd been in a funk and that she'd helped him out of it. Then she realized that he wasn't going to. Maybe he might manage to admit it later, once he'd come down from the high he was on, but for now, Tara was going to be left on her own to take the blame. How infuriating was that?

But Chloe had noticed something.

"What's that you've got?" she asked curiously.

Tara looked at the thing Sebastian had thrust into her hands. It was a beautiful notebook, quite large, and covered in brown leather. It was far too good for scribbling down ideas, but would be perfect for making copies of her finished songs. She opened it up. Inside there were two flaps, holding extra sheets of loose paper.

She looked at her fellow band members. There was Charlie, full of his own importance now he'd got over his fright, and the others, totally in the dark, and more than a little puzzled. Why should she have to explain what had happened? Trust Charlie to let her down after all she'd done for him.

For a moment Tara thought she was going to feel angry, but to her surprise, she didn't. Her main feeling was pride. Tara felt really proud that she'd helped Charlie through his fear. The gig could have been a total disaster, and yet it had ended up a triumph. And there was another feeling fluttering through her too, a feeling she'd been waiting and hoping for.

Then, to Tara's amazement, Charlie came over to her and gave her a big, bearlike hug, almost squeezing the life out of her.

"Thanks, Tara," he whispered, before punching the air in delight.

Tara ran her hands through her short, black hair. *Well,* she thought. *Perhaps he's not totally bad after all.*

But there was no time to think about that. "Has anyone got a pen?" she asked, taking out a piece of paper, and smoothing it onto the cover of her new notebook. "I've just had a brilliant idea for a song!"

✳ So you want
to be a pop star?
✳

Turn the page to read some top tips
on how to make your dreams
✳ come true... ✳

✹ Making it in the music biz ✹

Think you've got tons of talent?
Well, music maestro Judge Jim Henson,
Head of Rock at top talent academy Rockley
Park, has put together his hot tips to help
you become a superstar…

✹ Number One Rule: Be positive!
You've got to believe in yourself.

✹ Be active! Join your school choir
or form your own band.

 Be different! Don't be afraid to stand
out from the crowd.

✹ Be determined! Work hard and stay focused.

✹ Be creative! Try writing your own material –
it will say something unique about you.

✹ Be patient! Don't give up if things
don't happen overnight.

 Be ready to seize opportunities
when they come along.

Be versatile! Don't have a one-track mind – try out new things and gain as many skills as you can.

 Be passionate! Don't be afraid to show some emotion in your performance.

Be sure to watch, listen and learn all the time.

Be willing to help others.
You'll learn more that way.

Be smart! Don't neglect your schoolwork.

 Be cool and don't get big-headed! Everyone needs friends, so don't leave them behind.

Always stay true to yourself.

And finally, and most importantly, enjoy what you do!

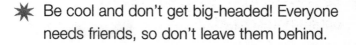

 Go for it! It's all up to you now...

Usborne Quicklinks

For links to exciting websites where you can find out more about becoming a pop star and even practise your singing with online karaoke, go to the Usborne Quicklinks Website at www.usborne-quicklinks.com and enter the keywords fame school.

Internet safety

When using the Internet make sure you follow these safety guidelines:

 Ask an adult's permission before using the Internet.

 Never give out personal information, such as your name, address or telephone number.

 If a website asks you to type in your name or e-mail address, check with an adult first.

 If you receive an e-mail from someone you don't know, do not reply to it.

For another fix of

read

Dancing Star

1 Some Exciting News

"Marmalade?"

Marmalade wasn't paying attention. He quite often had problems concentrating, and just now he was miles away. The five other students in the dance class had been paying close attention to what their teacher was saying, but Marmalade was thinking about how funny his biology teacher had looked when she walked into assembly this morning. It was something to do with the way she rolled her feet a bit sideways as she moved her weight from one foot to the other. Marmalade was well known for his mimicry, and he couldn't resist thinking about trying this walk. He knew it would make his classmates laugh if he could get it right…

"Marmalade!"

He jumped as Mr. Penardos shouted at him. "Sorry. I didn't hear what you were saying," Marmalade apologized quickly. But his dance teacher wasn't fooled.

"You didn' hear because you weren' listening," complained Mr. Penardos crossly. "I think per'aps I won' tell you, and you will miss out on this exciting chance."

"What chance?" Marmalade was paying attention now! "Do you think I'm in with a chance of being the next prom king?"

Mr. Penardos smiled. He never stayed cross for long, and he liked Marmalade Stamp. In spite of his periodic daydreaming, and the fact that he was the class clown, Marmalade was a very rewarding dancer to teach.

"I don' know abou' that," he said. "I was telling the class abou' the scout tha' is coming in a couple of days time."

"Scout? What for?" asked Marmalade. His friend and fellow dancer, Jack, groaned.

"It's a company called M & L Productions. They're casting a new pop video, and are looking for dancers," Jack explained. "We've already been through all this while you were staring out of the window."

"Sorry," said Marmalade again, excitement rippling through his mind. "That is good news. Who's the singer?"

"I don' have any news abou' the singer yet," said Mr. Penardos. "The production company is keeping the name secret at the moment."

"Why would they do that?" asked Jack in a puzzled voice.

"They might wan' to have a big build up and launch for the video," suggested Mr. Penardos. "And if details got ou' too soon it could ruin the effect. After all, these days, spoiler articles can get put ou' so quickly on the internet. There's no point in having a big launch if everyone already knows what you're doing."

"Wouldn't it be brilliant to get chosen?" said Marmalade. "I'd love to be in on a big secret. I wouldn't give it away, however much the media tried to bribe me."

"You're such a dreamer you probably wouldn't remember who it was even if you did get offered a bribe," said Martin, another dancer in the class.

Everyone laughed, including Marmalade. He didn't mind being teased, especially as Martin was probably right. By now, it was the end of the lesson. Marmalade picked up his towel, slung it round his neck and said goodbye to the girls. Ellie, Megan and Alice were heading off to their boarding house to shower and get changed, and the boys needed to do the same.

"See you at tea," he said to Alice.

"If you remember to turn up for it," she joked as she headed out of the door.

There was some free time before tea, and the boys chatted after they'd showered. "Are you going to go for this video job if we get the chance?" Marmalade asked the others. He paused outside the room he shared with Danny, Ed and Ben.

"Of course!" said Jack, and Martin nodded his agreement.

"We'd be daft not to," said Martin, leaning against

the doorpost. "Think about it. We'd earn money! These jobs can pay quite well."

Marmalade and Jack laughed. It was Martin's dream to buy a Porsche once he was eighteen, but he had a very long way to go before he had saved anything like enough money to do that!

"So you just want to do it for the car fund," teased Marmalade. "Have you got enough to buy a wing mirror yet?"

"You wait," said Martin. "If you get into the pop video circuit it's brilliant. My uncle told me. One job can lead to another and before you know it…yellow Porsche, leather seats, everything! And my uncle says the experience is really good too," he added. "You can get to meet some important people."

Martin's uncle was in America at the moment appearing in a show on Broadway, and he'd danced in several cool films as well. It was hard, making a living as a dancer, so the small number of dance students in Martin's year hung on his every word when he spoke about his uncle.

"Well I'm up for it," said Marmalade. "It sounds great."

"Me too," said Jack. "We need to take every chance we get in this business."

"So what's the best way to prepare?" asked Marmalade.

Martin grinned at Marmalade. "I'm not telling you that!" he said. "It's every man for himself as far as this job is concerned!"

To find out what happens next read

 Dancing Star

Cindy Jefferies' varied career has included being a Venetian-mask maker and a video DJ. Cindy decided to write *Fame School* after experiencing the ups and downs of her children, who have all been involved in the music business. Her insight into the lives of wannabe pop stars and her own musical background means that Cindy knows how exciting and demanding the quest for fame and fortune can be.

Cindy lives on a farm in Gloucestershire, where the animal noises, roaring tractors and rehearsals of Stitch, her son's indie-rock band, all help her write!

To find out more about Cindy Jefferies, visit her website: www.cindyjefferies.co.uk